Sight

Alexandria Clarimond

CEDRIC D. FISHER & COMPANY
PUBLISHERS

Editor:	Lola M. Fisher
Cover and Editorial Designer:	Sandra Schwartzman

ISBN eBook	979-8-9922459-8-1
ISBN Hardback	979-8-9922459-6-7
ISBN Paperback	979-8-9922459-9-8

Contents

Dedication

This story is dedicated to all the people living in this world who are confronting the challenges of living with degenerative retinal disease

Chronology of Loss

Event 1

A teenage girl tells her middle-aged mother, who wears bifocal glasses, "I will never have to wear glasses."

Event 2

An optometrist informs the female in her early forties during an eye examination for reading glasses, "You have a bad case of macular drusen. You will have serious sight problems later in life."

Event 3

A retina specialist informs the sixty-two-year-old female, "You have wet macular degeneration in the right eye; we need to start eye injections. The left eye has dry macular degeneration and will not need injections now."

Event 4

The woman, now seventy-one years old, receives a non-traditional eye treatment. After one year, she began receiving injections for wet macular degeneration in her left eye.

Event 5

The retina specialist informs the seventy-seven-year-old female that the macular degeneration "has advanced to geographic atrophy."

Event 6

At eighty years of age, the female has no central vision and is declared legally blind.

Event 7

Sight!

Prologue

Her thoughts drifted to the realization that she would soon acknowledge her 81st birthday. Her birthday celebrations ceased to occur many birthdays ago, as she had no one with whom to celebrate. Unable to sleep during the night, she decided to get out of bed, get dressed, eat her morning cereal, and fill the remaining time reflecting on how she has spent the years of her life. Not knowing what lay ahead, she neatly packed the personal items she was permitted to take to her appointment today. Now, she waits for the young doctor to arrive.

Dawn is beginning to spread its light through the small window of the living area of the tiny apartment where she resides. It would be a stretch to refer to it as the place where she lives. She does not live here; she exists here. The noises of the day have not yet awakened, creating a sense of solitude.

She has lived a rich life spanning the complete spectrum of emotional experiences, culminating in an unparalleled peace of mind that anyone can achieve. Her only regret is not having captured her life in a book before her vision became compromised, and now she can no longer read, write, drive a car, or see anyone's face. Her countless travel journals, blogs, and diaries would have formed its foundation. As she has progressed through the mental journey manifested in linear time on Earth, she remembers the family, friends, and acquaintances who have come into her life, leaving her with priceless good and bad memories. She recalls that she was preoccupied with the requirements for living on this planet for the first five decades of her life. She spent the remaining decades searching for and finally finding her preordained path, and felt blessed by the realization. She accommodated the loss of her vision, and for each major setback, she has improvised a solution to compensate. As the loss has progressed, she remains hopeful that if she can retain what vision remains, she can achieve a semi-normal life; however, each expectation has resulted in another decline. She lives a life convinced that losing sight does not mean losing one's life

Part I: Life is Good

Chapter One
- The Ball is in Your Court

"I will prepare, and some day my chance will come."
— Abraham Lincoln

Elora, referred to as Ellie by those who knew her, experienced a life with all her senses working in synchronicity for about seven decades. She enjoyed all the gifts her world presented to her. Then, a slow degenerative eye disease would present a life-altering event, proving to be the greatest challenge of her life.

Ellie was a shy, introverted child who felt comfortable being mostly alone, sharing her time with only her immediate family. Part of her personality formulation can be attributed to her family's life on a small farm until she was eight. There was no interaction with other children, as the closest neighbor with children was two miles away. But maybe there was another, more esoteric reason for her behavior.

As her mother used to tell it, Ellie died when she was just a few months old. Her crib was next to a window that encapsulated the view of a large sycamore tree a few yards from the house. Early one evening, a powerful thunderstorm developed in northeast Texas, producing thunder and lightning. A lightning bolt struck very close to the tree, causing Ellie to stop breathing. Although she did not know what the procedure was, her mother performed CPR on that frail little body. Eventually, Ellie started breathing again.

A barbed wire fence separated the small farm property and the larger neighboring farm up the road. The neighboring family was wealthy, at least that was what her father said; they had indoor plumbing and a television. They would sometimes ask Ellie and the family over on Sunday night to watch television. It was such a treat. One day, when Ellie, her mother, and sister, Carole, were doing laundry in the old wash tub in the backyard, something caught her eye. It was a wagon pulled by a team of healthy-looking horses, handled by the neighbor as he moved along the property fence line. Ellie followed the wagon to see where it was going as she disappeared from the backyard. Ellie's mother, sister, and the neighbor's wife quickly organized a small search party to look for her. The party soon caught sight of the neighbor driving the wagon and decided to get his assistance. When the party approached the wagon, they saw a small person slowly walking behind it. It was three-year-old, no-fear Ellie. She just wanted to discover where the wagon would lead her.

The family rarely traveled; they only went a relatively short distance when they did. A small child would consider forty miles a trip to the moon. One special outing was a visit to Ellie's favorite uncle, a few miles away. He was a quiet man, gentle, kind, and intelligent. He had books and magazines all over his house. Even before she could read, Ellie could be found in a secluded corner flipping through magazines, looking at the pictures. Magazines and books were not a commodity that the family could afford. Ellie never recalled her mother or father reading to her. Another favorite outing was to visit her favorite aunt. She was short, stout, funny, and an excellent cook. They spent every Thanksgiving enjoying the feast she made, and she always made fried peach pies for Ellie and her brother.

Ellie's world revolved around her secure home and family. From childhood into high school, Ellie excelled in all subjects; however, her education did not start well. The small school district in which she lived did not include kindergarten, so knowledge of the ABCs was lacking as the time approached for the first grade. When the school bus pulled up to let her board, sudden panic struck her, and she refused to get on. Her sister, Carole, tried to coax her onto the bus, but she would not budge. The bus driver attempted to calm her down unsuccessfully. The other kids on the bus started laughing and made fun of her. Carole gave up and found a seat. Finally, her mother came out and lifted Ellie onto the bus steps, the door closed, and the bus left.

A feeling of abandonment paralyzed her. Where was

she going? Who was going to take care of her? Why were all the kids laughing? She does not remember how she managed to find a seat. She sat alone until the bus arrived at school. She does not remember much of what happened that first day of school; only that somehow everything turned out all right and the fear left her at some point.

Frequent nosebleeds plagued Ellie during the first few years of her life, but she never experienced one while in school. One spring day, as all the kids lined up to catch their school bus home, blood came pouring from her nose, a trickle at first, then a rapid stream. Her teacher rushed Ellie to the bathroom and applied wet compresses to her nose until the blood flow stopped. While all this was happening, the school bus had been loaded and left. She felt afraid and began to cry, wondering how she would get home. Her teacher drove her home, and from that day forward, her second-grade teacher remained her favorite teacher. She never had another nosebleed at school.

The exposure to cruelty by her classmates continued, manifesting itself in their teasing of Ellie because she wore ugly shoes. Born with a deformed right foot, her mother gave her daily foot massages as an infant and bought high-top, lace-up leather shoes as a toddler. Ellie wore those ugly shoes through the second grade. Her mother, through home therapy and ugly shoes, straightened her foot to the point where it looked normal. The home therapy and ugly shoes also improved her walking gait. Through the years, she avoided sports requiring quick, agile ankle movements since her right ankle was subject to turning very easily, causing painful sprains lasting for days.

This experience, in conjunction with the fact that she wore dresses that were homemade from flour sacks, awakened her to the fact that she was not like most of the kids in school. She and her family were poor. Ellie began understanding why the family had no birthday parties and lived in a three-room shack without running water and plumbing. Living on a small farm, her playmate was her younger brother, Lee; there was no interaction with other kids their age. Her sister, seven years older than her, ignored her, especially since she had chores to do. The assimilation of all this information resulted in diminished self-confidence, as evidenced by her habit of always wearing a coat over her dress at school, which was another source of ridicule from her classmates. The coat was her safety blanket.

Lee was her only true friend during the farm years. Older by two years, Ellie flaunted her age and size over him, taking advantage of every opportunity to tease him. As the years passed, he began to fight back, so to speak, first by tattling on Ellie to their mother and eventually, he fought back physically. Their favorite place to play was in the dirt backyard where all the chickens ran around. She made a couple of mud pies and tried to convince him to eat them. He refused, and when she moved the pie toward his mouth, he quickly hit her across the bridge of her nose with a small bucket. Pain struck Ellie like she had never experienced, and blood started gushing from her nose and pouring down her throat. Her screaming brought their mother outside. After explaining their version of the story, their mother did not punish either. Ellie, of course, thought Lee should have been punished for hitting her in the nose, never admitting she started the whole situation. She had a scar across the bridge of her nose until she was in her twenties.

A particularly memorable setback occurred during the summer school vacation between the first and second grades. When Ellie returned to school for the second grade, her teacher put her in the slow reading group. Her vision was not a problem. Instead, it was the lack of reading material to reinforce the reading skills she had already achieved. This humiliating and embarrassing event motivated Ellie to work harder, and within six weeks, she had rejoined the regular group. Her teacher never sent her to the back of the class again. Studying became a passion, resulting in academic success, thus endearing her to her mother and teachers. Always curious, she favored science and mathematics as these subjects allowed her mind to solve problems.

The summer after the second grade, Ellie's daddy sold the farm and found a job in town. The family moved, and from third grade through high school, she began to emerge from her self-induced cocoon.

Chapter Two – Sight Loss Event 1

"Sight is the noblest sense of man."
— Albrecht Durer

The move to town was a life-altering event that brought positive changes for the entire family. The basic need for shelter was overwhelmingly satisfied. They moved into a comfortable, brick, three-bedroom house with plumbing and running water. They enjoyed the cool breeze from a window air conditioner during the hot, humid summers. It was many months before Ellie realized they had moved into government-subsidized housing. Still absent was the new home entertainment equipment, a television. But, since they never had one, how could they miss it? Without the constant attention required by the farm, the time devoted to physical labor decreased significantly, freeing up hours for leisure activities, such as playing, reading, outdoor activities, and games. Neighbors were closer, maybe too close. Ellie embraced all the wonderful things happening to her, and that's how it would be for the next twenty years or so. She became a different person in many ways; she was developing her mind, body, and soul for the next big step.

Ellie loved recess and gym classes; in those days, the schools had no intramural athletics for girls. Had there been, she would have spent time on the basketball court, a sport her mother excelled in. She kept the old photograph of her mother and the other members of her high school team who won the state championship in 1926. Occasionally, she would pull out the photograph and look at it for encouragement. Just recently, she looked at the photo, and her thoughts revolved around all the changes in the world she had witnessed to date. The baggy, heavy bloomers with flowing sailor collar tops and high-top leather shoes her mother and teammates wore had been replaced by synthetic, lightweight, moisture-repellent tops, shorts, and lightweight fabric sports shoes, all designed to enhance the performance of athletes.

Financially, the family status was improving. When Ellie's mother got a job, there was enough money to buy new furniture, store-bought clothes, and even piano lessons. Ellie's sister was a pianist at the church, and her mother wanted Ellie to focus on learning to play church hymns so Ellie could take her sister's place as church pianist when the time came. During three years of learning classical music, Ellie balked when her mother demanded she start learning hymns: "If you don't learn to play church music, then no more lessons." Ellie said, "Fine, no more lessons." Such defiance came as a surprise to her mother. She was surprised that Ellie was standing up for herself. During this time of material abundance, her mother began to wear bifocal glasses that were compliant with a prescription; she no longer had to wear cheap readers. Ellie cannot remember when her mother did not wear glasses. One day, her mother complained about how bad her vision was getting. Ellie impolitely told her, "I will never have to wear glasses."

Ellie's academic achievements continued throughout her public school education. She felt challenged by competent, caring teachers. Success through this venue earned the respect of her classmates; success in making friends ensured her selection as the female senior class favorite. She had overcome the shyness and insecurity exhibited in the first few years of her life. She even had the rare opportunity to meet a world-renowned scientist due to one exceptional achievement she accomplished while a sophomore in high school.

At that time, an organization was sponsoring student essay contests nationwide, with the subject of Communism. Ellie's English teacher asked her and another classmate to enter the competition. At that time, the internet was not available, so she did research at both the school library and the city library. Ellie's essay won first place in the state, while the other student placed second. What are the odds of two students from the same grade, attending the same school, placing first and second in a writing contest? Their accomplishments illustrate the quality of teaching at that school. The school submitted the essays for the national competition, where Ellie placed 10th and the other student placed fifth.

The organization sponsoring the contest introduced the winners at an annual national conference in Houston, Texas. Two teachers drove Ellie and the other student to the event. They met and talked to the guest speaker, Dr.

Edward Teller, who many refer to as the father of the hydrogen bomb. At the conference, he spoke of the advances in nuclear medicine. Of course, Ellie did not understand what he was saying and had never heard of this person before. However, decades later, she realized she had met and talked to a very important person when she was young. Not bad, for a country bumpkin.

Graduating as valedictorian of her senior class ensured Ellie's entrance into the college of her choice. Her goal was to teach high school science. Her mentor had encouraged her to teach science. She selected a small teachers' university in northeast Texas. A small scholarship, a student loan, and working as a waitress were necessary to complete college. Her parents were not financially capable of supporting her higher education. During graduate school, she taught science labs at the university. At the end of five years, Ellie received her Master's in Science Degree with a double major in biology and chemistry. She taught middle school science for five years in a town near the university.

Chapter Three
- Introduction to Religion

"Religion is the clearest telescope through which we can behold the beauties of creation."
—William Scott Downey

Within a couple of months of the move to town, Ellie's mother, with kids in tow, started attending a small church just across the street from their house. Her family had never attended church. Life gave her a new learning experience since she did not know what church was; what was she supposed to do or say? Her daddy never went to church. The only time Ellie saw him in church was at the funeral home chapel when he passed away. Her mother was determined to raise the kids according to God's law, which would provide a moral foundation for their lives. Therefore, her mother and the kids would attend services every Sunday morning and evening. They attended Wednesday night prayer meetings. They also attended special events like week-long revivals, summer Bible school, choir events, and Christmas programs.

Religion became essential to Ellie, providing her with core values she would retain for the rest of her life. She made many friends in her Sunday school class who provided social outlets outside of church, such as sleepovers, going to movies, sharing Sunday dinner after church, and sharing clothes. Ellie especially liked singing in the choir; she was the best alto. This talent exhibited itself during a talent show hosted by the school district. Partnering with a friend in her Sunday school class, they dressed up like hobos, and although their rendition of "Gotta Travel On" received a warm reception and laughter at their costumes, they did not win. However, they had fun, and Ellie built up her courage to confront the audience. Could that song possibly become her theme song in life? She appreciated the women who volunteered to teach the Sunday school lessons, but she was afraid she was becoming an irritant to them.

After two or three years of religious indoctrination, Ellie began to think for herself and ask questions. In her mind, God was not to be feared; he was love and kindness, and brought peace and joy. Hellfire and brimstone were not ideas to which she was receptive. She often asked questions to which the teacher responded, "You just have to have faith." That got old after a while. The church taught strict adherence to God's word. Ellie dared not mention things like spirituality, reincarnation, or enlightened masters. She became unfulfilled and frustrated with the church and organized religion. When Ellie left home at eighteen to attend college, she became an agnostic and followed that path for approximately four decades.

Chapter Four
- Visions of Friendship and Love

"Friendship at first sight, like love at first sight, is said to be the only truth."
—Herman Melville

Ellie made friends easily in the neighborhood where the family had moved. She learned to be respectful of others while speaking her mind when needed; learning personality types that suited her became essential in forming friendships. On summer nights, she and Lee would meet with several other children after supper to play softball, build mini houses in the dirt, ride bikes, and chase the city truck spraying DDT to kill mosquitoes. During the day, when the temperature was hot, they would play cards or board games and read funny books. The ease of making friends transcended when she started third grade at the end of summer. Ellie felt more confident now, more "normal." The remaining years of school would be promising, she thought.

Families in her hometown rarely took vacations; they could not afford them, and people did not travel that much then. One exception was Ellie's best friend forever, Joyce, and her parents. They invited her to a week-long summer vacation to Hot Springs, Arkansas. Ellie had never left Texas, so going to Arkansas was like going to the moon. Ellie and Joyce sometimes wore identical clothes made by Joyce's mother. She was like another child to them; Ellie considered Joyce's mother her second mother. Ellie still has an old photo of them dressed as twins walking the streets of Hot Springs. The scenery was beautiful and mountainous. One day, as they traversed a mountain with twists and turns in the road, Ellie said, "Haven't we passed this before?" Everyone laughed. Ellie had a wonderful time, and this experience increased her appetite for more travel, which came to fruition later in life.

A few years after the move to town, Ellie was surprised when she seemed to take a greater interest in the male gender, other than just someone with whom to ride bicycles. Even though she had many boyfriends, the relationships never lasted long, as someone else would come along whom she found to be more interesting. She had her first date with her first real boyfriend in seventh grade. He was cute and talkative; his parents were financially better off than hers. One Saturday afternoon, he and his dad picked her up to see a movie. The nervous twosome sat in the back seat of the car, never saying a word to each other. The theater had a balcony, and of course, that is where all the couples liked to sit. Ellie and her beau sat in the balcony, but neither was experienced in courtship and did not take advantage of the setting. He invited her to his birthday party at his house.

They played games about which she was clueless, like coupling up and walking around the house, or playing spin the bottle. Yes, the parents chaperoned the party guests; however, his parents were more receptive to supervised exploration. Ellie's mother was pacing the floor back home the entire time, nervous about her decision to let Ellie go on a date at such a young age. It would be one of many times her mother paced the floor when she was on a date. Ellie named her nervous Nellie, never understanding the cause of her mother's emotional state.

A couple of years later, Ellie met a boy named Russell at the roller skating rink located in a neighboring town. She and Joyce went skating every Saturday night for a couple of years. Her second mother always drove them and ensured no promiscuity occurred from anyone. Russell was a superb skater; he could skate backwards and even dance on skates. The couple skated to almost every song; Joyce eventually found a male partner, as she was getting tired of skating alone. The two couples double-dated sometimes. As time passed, Ellie discovered he was a couple of years older and a quarterback on the football team. He invited her to a football banquet, where he received an award. Her mother made her a beautiful light blue satin dress for the occasion. When she and Russell entered the room, all eyes were on them. She felt like royalty being with him. Because they lived in different towns, they communicated primarily through mail and occasional phone calls. She discovered Russell also had a bad boy reputation. After a year or so, the relationship fizzled due to distance and Ellie's reluctance to devote more time to someone with a questionable reputation. However, he was always a perfect gentleman with her.

Next up was Larry, who later would become her husband. Larry and Ellie dated for the last two and a half years of high school. They complied with societal expectations that high school sweethearts get married after high school graduation, have kids, and she would be a stay-at-home mom. However, Ellie had other plans; her focus throughout high school was getting good grades. She and Larry broke up, but they got back together. After high school, she attended college, the first in her immediate and extended family to do so. Intuition compelled her to forgo marriage after high school, even though Ellie and Larry were engaged by this time. He did not want to pursue a college education, so he worked while she pursued a higher education. This arrangement lasted a year, then they broke up again.

On her way to class one morning, Ellie passed by a site where a car accident had occurred. She observed that one of the automobiles belonged to Larry. Emergency personnel had already taken him to the hospital; she skipped class and went to the hospital to see how he was. His injuries were not serious, and he recovered within a week or so. This experience drew them back together, and they secretly married a few months later. Why secretly? Ellie knew her mother did not want her to get married until she received her college degree. The following fall, Ellie transferred to another university. Larry got a job, they bought a house, and started their life together. He offered emotional support for Ellie's higher education endeavor but did not contribute financial aid toward her expenses. Larry wanted children; she wanted to finish her education and start her teaching career.

Inevitably, the marriage ended after seven and a

half years. Larry began an affair with one of her good friends, but did not have the courage to ask for a divorce. He would not give up the other woman. Ellie knew she could not live with that situation, so she told him to get a lawyer, and she would not contest the divorce. Ellie was very hurt by the infidelity, and it took her about two years to even think about dating seriously again. After a few years, she knew the marriage could have only ended this way. They were just kids with different values and perspectives on life when they married. They had a special relationship, but not a holy one. The adverse emotional impact of the divorce and unlearning circumstances would have a lasting influence on her life; this life-altering event would result in doors opening for her that she could never imagine.

Ellie would continue the path destined just for her. She knew that remaining in the same town with her ex and his new wife, working in a career that promised a non-livable income, and participation in an environment that provided no mental or physical stimulation, would not lead her in the right direction. At that time, the United States Department of Defense was actively recruiting females to serve in several positions previously closed to women. After speaking with recruiters of all military service branches, Ellie committed to serving as an officer in one of them. In four months, she would report for basic training. She had broken free of everything that could potentially hold her back.

She developed some lasting friendships with males that were not romantic. She was fortunate to learn that she did not have to be in a romantic relationship; genuine, caring friendships can occur between the genders.

Chapter Five
- Life is A Beach

"At the beach, life is different.
Time doesn't move hour to hour, but mood to moment.
We live by the currents, plan by the tides, and follow the sun."
—Sandy Gingras

Ellie spent the last chapter of her old life at the beach sowing wild oats during the summer before she had to report for basic training. Joan, her friend in this adventure, taught English in the same middle school where Ellie taught science. Joan became Ellie's teacher in refining her living experience. She learned how to choose clothing that would enhance her physique, use colors to complement her skin tone, and move gracefully when walking to flaunt what she had. She improved her dining out etiquette and selection of restaurants. She learned how to listen to people and respond to them politely. Thanks to Joan, Ellie developed into a lady, a trait that would become a positive attribute of her personality.

Joan was Ellie's lifeline during the divorce period. She helped her adjust to life without a husband. Joan was also divorced and a single parent to a wonderful little boy, Jeffrey. She became Ellie's role model in lifting herself and getting on with life after a setback. They packed the needed household items and moved into a two-bedroom apartment on the street opposite the beach. Nearly every day in the late morning, they would head to the beach, spend a few hours basking in the sun, and watch all the guys as they walked by. Joan, the extrovert, could start a conversation with a perfect stranger, especially if he was pleasing to the eye. Ellie always envied that ability; she, an introvert, would come out of her shell only after a few pina coladas. They would check out the bar scene several nights a week.

Jeffrey spent the summer with his grandparents when he was not with Joan. Through her parentage, he was always polite and mature beyond his age. When he spent days with Joan, the three of them would go to the beach during the day and watch television in the evening. Sometimes, Joan would get a babysitter, allowing her to go out for the evening. One evening when Joan had a date, Ellie babysat. With Joan's permission, they went to see "Jaws." Super inquisitive, Jeffrey asked many questions during the movie. She was impressed that he did not seem to be afraid. Yet, after they got home and were ready for bed, he asked Ellie if he could sleep with her until Joan got home. Ellie has always thought of him when she has seen the movie numerous times over the years.

Realizing that she needed to be mentally and physically ready for basic training, Ellie would spend many mornings walking or biking along the beach, gradually building up to a slow jog. Mentally, she was ready; she knew academics would be no problem. She knew the military would build her physically, but did not want to start at ground zero.

Joan and Ellie met two male friends with whom they occasionally went out. Ellie found it refreshing that there was no commitment since she would leave in a few months. Joan had a visit once from an old relationship, a coach at the school where they had worked. During the evening, an argument ensued; Joan ran out the front door with him in pursuit. Ellie stalled him for a few minutes, trying to calm him, but it did not work. She told frightened Jeffrey to stay put; she followed Joan and her coach friend outside to determine the level of anger in the two of them. Joan was halfway across an open field to the beach when the coach rapidly approached. The chase ended when Ellie yelled for them to stop, but they remained outside, discussing the matter. Ellie went back to Jeffrey and watched TV. Joan terminated her romance with the coach, opening another door to her future husband. She also met a beach friend with whom she established a relationship, but it also ended, widening the door for Joan to proceed with another relationship. Next, Ellie dated the brother of Joan's beach friend; she counseled him as he was on the rebound from an airline flight attendant. Then she dated a medical student who taught her some things about the human body.

Ellie had never felt so free to do anything without someone judging her, knowing there was nothing to keep her there. The months passed quickly, and soon it was time to head to basic training. Joan decided not to return to the old teaching position and accepted a position closer to the beach. They both were looking for something then, but did not find it until after they said goodbye. It was an excellent time for Ellie; she always thought of it fondly. She continued to love the cathartic effect of the beach and traveled to many beaches in her life.

Chapter Six
- Lady Blue

"The cars we drive say a lot about us."
— Alexandra Paul

The next decade or so was, without exception, a time of unimagined personal joy, emotional pain, mental growth, and career productivity, which provided a solid foundation for the last years of Ellie's life. Lady Blue was the name of the car she owned and drove for fourteen years.

When she first saw Lady Blue, a 1976 sky blue Datsun 280Z, in the showroom of the Maryland car dealership, the sleek, compact, eye-catching form immediately caught her attention. She knew she had to own this car. Ignoring societal conditioning, Ellie bought the Japanese-produced sports car. No more frumpy American-made sedans for her. Ellie knew her Ford and Chevy relatives and friends would think she had lost her mind buying this car, believing it to be a cheap, poorly constructed car that would probably soon fall apart. Time proved them wrong in many ways; most of her relatives and friends now own Japanese-made cars. Most importantly, Ellie changed her thinking, unafraid to disregard what people thought if she perceived a threat to her desires, and continued a pattern of similar non-conformist actions.

A few years after the purchase, Ellie's fiancé wanted to buy personalized plates with "Lady Blue" on them. But California already had a car license plate with that name. So, he used the French equivalent, "Mme Bleu," and the license plate displayed that name for the next ten years. Lady Blue and Ellie traveled across the country a few times, experienced many adventures, and had a lot of fun driving the winding roads of Mount Tamalpais on Sunday road trips from Sausalito to Stinson Beach and Bodega Bay. They took care of each other. Lady Blue was the personification of Ellie for fourteen years of her life.

Ellie's mind was undergoing many changes. She had experienced events leading her down a new path that was not always popular with others. She was the first in her immediate or extended family to get a college degree. She was the first in her family to get a divorce. She quit a secure teaching career. She entered the military, which tripled her salary, and disgraced the family. She was developing into a person alien to all who knew her. With all the opposition to her life decisions, the only thing left for her to do was keep on going.

Several months before purchasing Lady Blue, Ellie began her new career in the military, first attending basic and officer branch training. Basic training in Alabama flew by, and she had never been so tired. Each weekday training included physical training, weapons training, military academic subjects, and even officer etiquette training. The first day she signed into the unit, the training officers informed her that she would be responsible for "charge of quarters" duty that night. This responsibility meant she had to stay awake all night, conduct periodic security checks, and handle any emergencies that might arise. A precise log of each of her actions was maintained as required. When she was relieved from duty the next morning, the company commander was surprised at the thoroughness of the log. Her teaching skills contributed to this tiny success.

When Ellie arrived on the first day, she received her issue of uniforms, which included more ugly shoes called "grannies." She always had trouble breaking in new shoes; blisters would form on both heels, which required time to heal before the shoes became comfortable. She did not get the opportunity to break in the grannies before the night duty, and blisters formed. When walking in formation to class the next morning, Ellie's heels were burning, but she kept marching and blotted the pain out of her mind. She felt someone pull her out of formation; it was the company commander, a tough African American woman from the streets of Detroit. The commander immediately took her to sick call, where they treated her feet to alleviate the pain. Her heels were raw and bleeding. Ellie was allowed to wear tennis shoes for about three weeks, but she wore the grannies in the evening to break them in. The photographer took the class photo and placed her in the back row so her tennis shoes would not show.

The toughness Ellie exhibited, marching with bleeding heels, earned the respect of the company commander. The superior officer referred to her as an informal leader.

Of course, Ellie could never form a friendship with her superior officer, but they did have drinks during a social event toward the end of the course. One week after graduating from the Army basic course, Ellie attended the officer specialty course.

It was winter by then, and the wind blowing across the Chesapeake Bay into the post where she would live and attend school for the following nine months was colder than any she had experienced. Ellie learned how to dress for the cold weather, a necessity when participating in training maneuvers. She worried about Lady Blue sitting out in the cold, wet rain, and snow. Both survived. Springtime in Maryland was beautiful. Mother Nature was attired in her most exquisite colors and presented Ellie with idyllic weather most suited for short road trips with the window down in her new sports car on weekends. During the week, she devoted herself to studying to complete the military course, ensuring that the day would come when she would report to her first duty assignment. Studying always came easily for Ellie, and it was a priority in her life, as she was on the brink of embarking upon an atypical career path. She wanted not only to perform well but also to thrive in a new environment.

The months flew by. Ellie completed the course. Soon, military orders were in hand for her first assignment in California. Of all the numerous routes Ellie could have taken to travel from Maryland to San Francisco, California, she chose a southern route to visit family in Texas and Arkansas on the way west. Since GPS was unavailable then, she had accumulated every road atlas and all state maps available for the coast-to-coast journey.

Ellie had a new, fun car and was eager to see how they would manage on this long road trip.

Chapter Seven
- California Bound

"If you're going to San Francisco, be sure to wear some flowers in your hair."
—John Phillips

Packing the car tested Ellie's organizational skills. Lady Blue was a two-seater with a small storage area behind the seats, under the hatchback. After planning and adjusting plans a few times, she finally got all the military gear, civilian clothes, books, and a small TV into a space approximately 36 cubic feet. All the maps and military documents occupied the passenger seat.

This trip to California was the first long road trip that Ellie would be taking alone. Of course, being young and inexperienced, she had no fear of all the possibilities for harm that might confront her along the journey. Planning the trip, securing accommodations along the route without reservations, servicing the car, navigating the path, and learning how to use commercial truck drafting to her advantage further bolstered her confidence. Daily distances varied from 500 to 600 miles. She took a few short breaks to fill up Lady Blue, eat food, and stretch unexercised muscles.

The first leg of the trip west was from Baltimore to a small town 100 miles east of Dallas off I-30, approximately 1,500 miles. She did not remember the location or lodging name for the first two nights, as she focused on the distance driven and an adequate, safe place to sleep for the night. Surprisingly, Ellie did not feel fatigued. Driving through the Deep South was uneventful and pleasant. She felt comfortable and at home, since the part of East Texas where she was born and raised, the termination of the first leg of the trip, is situated on the western fringe of the Deep South. As she passed through Georgia, she made a mental note to start a genealogy project for her father's lineage. His family migrated from Georgia to Texas in 1903. She began the genealogy project years later, tracing her roots to 1806. Her great-great-grandfather was a soldier in the unit that was the last defense of Atlanta when General Sherman blew through the Deep South during the Civil War. Life events interfered with her completion of the project.

On the third day, Lady Blue transported Ellie to her parents' house around suppertime. She did not want to return to East Texas, but felt obligated to visit her parents before settling into her new life in California. Her mother cooked her favorite meal—fresh pinto beans, cornbread, green onions, and fresh tomato slices. But

four hours later, she was ready to leave; Ellie did not know how to manage two days trying to converse with two people who did not understand why she was doing what she was doing. Old memories, responsible for her desire to leave this place and never return, bombarded her throughout the entire visit. For the first time in many months, Ellie felt deflated. Within the year, her father would die from a heart attack. She could never change her frame of mind during the visit. Later in life, she realized she had created the illusion that her parents did not love her.

Early the next morning, on day three, Ellie packed and was ready to leave; she said her farewells, promising to stay in touch. She departed, heading for Arkansas to visit Lee, nearly four hours north. She wanted to see him and his family and show off her new car. Born two years apart, they were close as children and enjoyed playing together. They also enjoyed playing with the neighborhood kids after moving to town. They were very competitive, especially with each other. Ellie also wanted to showcase the physical prowess that she had gained after all the military training and suggested a two-mile run around the nearby school track. Even though he had not been working out, he agreed. He made the run, but he was in pain at the end. Lee could never resist a challenge from her. Ellie stayed a couple of days reminiscing about the good old days. Only in her mind would the "good old days" be found in the future.

The second and longest leg of the trip would be about 2,000 miles long. The route would go west on I-40 through the Texas Panhandle, New Mexico, Arizona, and into California. She did not make hotel reservations anywhere along the way. The plan was to drive until she got tired, find a hotel, eat dinner, and crash for the night. Sightseeing was interspersed along the route, coinciding with rest and meal stops. With spirits lifted, Ellie looked forward to seeing the southwest part of the country, a foreign territory never seen except in movies.

The terrain slowly changed from lush vegetation in Arkansas to prairies and plains in Oklahoma. There were no large cities to speak of through which to navigate, just a pleasant, calming landscape. Ellie wondered what the people who lived there did for a living. What did they do for fun? What were their hopes and aspirations? The location where she chose to stop for the night, Albuquerque, New Mexico, was a little over 500 miles from Oklahoma City, but spending the night in the Texas Panhandle was not an option. The sun was beginning to set as she found lodging on the west side of town to avoid the commuter traffic when she headed west the following morning. There was no time for sightseeing here; there were still many more miles to go, and she had to report to the duty station in one week. Driving and stops consumed ten hours. She was tired and wanted a good night's sleep, thinking she would taper off a bit the next day. Ellie had no idea that a future assignment would bring her back to New Mexico and Sandia Peak for temporary duty, when there would be more time to see this beautiful place.

Waking up a little later than usual, Ellie decided breakfast would be the only meal until dinner time, snacking along the route. Kingman, AZ, would be the next stop; it was a little further than intended, but Flagstaff was not far enough. She thought she would spend more time in Flagstaff someday as she found it inviting from the drive through it. She would get her wish. The terrain was mostly desert for this stretch, and although beautiful, it became somewhat boring after about four hours.

Although spaciousness was preferable to the big cities, the southwestern part of the country would not be a preferred location to put down roots someday. Kingman was surprisingly busy, but Ellie found a hotel quickly, again as the sun was beginning to set. Dinner was Tex-Mex with a couple of Margaritas; was it the best she'd ever eaten, or was she just hungry and tired? After watching some nightly news, Ellie drifted into a very sound sleep.

The next leg of the journey presented an experience responsible for adjusting her no-fear inclination. Ellie stopped to fill up the car about 100 miles outside of Bakersfield. As she pulled out of the station, she noticed a tan vehicle leave the station behind her, about 500 feet from the rear of Lady Blue. The car followed her, matching her speed as she sped up and slowed down as a test to see if it would pass her; it never did. As she entered the city limits of Bakersfield, she pulled into a service station to see what the car would do. The car drove past. After about ten minutes, Ellie pulled onto the road and looked to see if the vehicle was following her. There was no sign of it. She continued until she reached the city limits on the other side of town, where she stopped for the night, unnerved from the incident. Ellie vowed to be more cautious and observe her surroundings, now acutely aware that the road for a female driving alone with out-of-state license plates could potentially be dangerous.

Ellie awoke the next morning feeling a little more secure, because it was the last piece of the trip. The driving time to San Francisco would be under five hours, if the traffic and road conditions cooperated. Excited, but nervous about driving in a big city, she talked with Lady Blue, telling her she needed her help. At Los Banos on I-5, she headed west to catch Highway 101, which leads to San Francisco. The traffic was not bad until San Jose, and then Ellie encountered the worst traffic she had ever experienced. Fighting the fear that she would never learn to drive in this congestion, she could sense her excitement and confidence fading. But an inner strength enveloped her, calming her mind and enabling her to navigate the city and over the Golden Gate Bridge. She found lodging just north of the bridge in Marin County, where she planned to rent an apartment. The long, arduous road journey was over. Ellie celebrated with drinks and a wonderful dinner. Tomorrow she would collect herself, prepare her uniform for duty the following day, and explore the neighborhood.

Chapter Eight
- A New Life

"All the world's a stage. And all the men and women merely players; they have their exits and their entrances, and one man in his time plays many parts...."
— William Shakespeare

All the military training during the past year prepared Ellie for this moment; the time to produce had arrived. She was satisfied that she had assembled her uniform according to the regulations for the occasion. She pressed her green dress uniform, correctly placed her name tag, and shined her low-heeled black pumps. Lady Blue and Ellie crossed the Golden Gate Bridge into San Francisco and entered the military post at approximately 8:00; traffic on the bridge was heavy. This trip was the first of many early commuter trips the two would make for almost three and a half years. She never tired of the majestic view of the bay every time she crossed. Finding the in-processing center was easy since it was not a large installation. She completed the signing-in process for the new assignment within a couple of hours. Ellie was introduced to her sponsor to help her get settled, find a place to live, and learn how to survive in the assignment, as one of the few women in uniform working at the installation.

Although she would miss her family and friends she had left behind, Ellie looked forward to making new friends, some of whom would become like family to her. When she met her sponsor, Bobbie, she knew they would become very good friends, sisters. They were both raised in small towns, relatively close to each other. Bobbie was dedicated and advanced her career in the Army to become the executive officer of the Garrison Headquarters Company. Over time, she introduced Ellie to many people who could help her advance to more challenging assignments. Ellie would learn much from Bobbie over the next couple of years.

However, Ellie first had to find a place to live. Bobbie suggested moving into the apartment complex where she lived, so Ellie lived with her briefly until she found a more suitable place, something close to the water. After they drove around for a few days after work and on weekends, Ellie finally found an apartment at the water's edge in Sausalito. It was terrific; she thought of it fondly long after she moved on to new assignments, and no other place compared to the ambiance of that first apartment in her new life. The water smashing against the shoreline rocks was melodic and induced immediate sleep at night. Watching sailboats in the bay from the patio became a favorite way to relieve stress after work. Located near several fabulous restaurants, Ellie and her frequent visitors looked forward to working through the restaurant menus.

The two friends spent much time together, taking weekend trips to vineyards, sightseeing nearby, and getting the lay of the land. They always traveled in Lady Blue because she was a fun car, although they could not put a lot of luggage or purchases in her. Lady Blue loved getting out on the road, exercising the engine and steering. Ellie even let Bobbie take the wheel now and then; however, Bobbie was not comfortable driving a stick shift, which meant Ellie did most of the driving, which was not unpleasant to her. At times on weekends, Ellie would go off by herself, especially to beach areas, which had a way of invigorating her soul after a few weeks of working a challenging job. She always welcomed the opportunity to be alone, to escape to a place where only peace filled her mind.

They also spent their leisure time going to parties and taking weekend trips to a military installation a couple of hours south, where they could meet men with whom they did not have a professional working relationship. Ellie dated one man for a short while, whom she met at the military installation. She was surprised she found the courage to tell him that the chemistry wasn't there, and she wanted to move on—a total reversal of her past behavior, barely a year ago. She had decided she did not want to remarry but devote her time to a career. And in any relationship, if she discovered that her male companion did not support that decision, Ellie would extend her well-wishes.

Ellie had several more beaus during this time. One taught her how to sail, one taught her how to disco dance, one opened her mind to hard rock music, and one exposed her to fine arts and the symphony. Ellie was at peace with her lackadaisical relationships with men. Even their marital status was of no concern to her. In her mind, there was no expectation from them; she did not want them to expect anything from her. There was only room for genuine appreciation for each other's company. She told herself, "Don't get too close." Then she met a man who began to collapse the wall Ellie had built around her heart.

He was tall, attractive, well-educated, intelligent, and well-established in a military career at the installation where she was assigned. Of course, Ellie was well guarded against all these pleasing traits. They enjoyed doing the same things, discussing numerous topics, and learning about each other. Ellie began seeing Bobbie less and less because Jason, her new man, consumed most of her time. They took weekend trips, attended concerts, went on wine country outings, and sightseeing, which provided opportunities for them to spend time together. She gradually considered that this relationship may be different from all the rest; maybe she should let her guard down and give it a chance. In a few short months, Ellie and Jason were considered a couple by all their friends and coworkers.

Nine months into the relationship, he told her that he had to go away for the upcoming weekend, explaining that he was going to visit an old friend, hospitalized after a mugging. The internal alarm immediately went off; she doubted his explanation. Ellie was all too familiar with lying and instantly knew when it occurred. Interrogation after his return from the weekend trip revealed that he had gone to a concert with an old girlfriend. Flooded with anger, disappointment, rejection, and abandonment, Ellie withdrew internally to determine how she would proceed with the relationship. After Jay apologized and said it would never happen again, she gave him a second chance.

A few months after this personal setback, Bobbie informed Ellie that she was leaving the military and returning to Louisiana to be near her family. Not sure this was the real reason for Bobbie's leaving the military, Ellie felt abandoned again. She was losing her good friend. After Bobbie left, they corresponded regularly, but the frequency of their communication decreased until it ceased altogether. Retracing memories, Ellie knew that friends would come and go; serve each other for a while, then go on to the next special relationship that crossed their path.

Meanwhile, the second chance with Jason eventually led to a third and fourth. Ellie knew the relationship with the man she was devoting her time, energy, and emotion to was toxic; she deserved better. When she received orders for a new assignment, despite his pleas for her to leave the military and stay with him, Ellie's inner strength and courage emerged, enabling her to go and continue to the next assignment. This second experience of betrayal by a man created a vacuum that she could never allow again. Lady Blue and Ellie would soon embark on another cross-country trip that would occupy her mind and ease her emotional state.

Personal life aside, Ellie acquired skills that prepared her for continued momentum in her career. She learned the proper way to write military correspondence, the value of networking with people, and expressing her opinion with favorable results despite the chain of command structure. Within two years of her assignment at the installation, she was selected for company command, becoming the first female to achieve this distinction. The leadership skills she learned and executed increased her confidence and earned her the respect of her superiors. Part of her responsibility was serving as the commander of troops during retirement ceremonies, executing commands with a military saber. Ellie had exceeded her expectations for success and looked forward to future assignments to build upon her accomplishments. Despite personal emotional pain, the time she spent in San Francisco was rewarding and a time she would fondly remember.

Chapter Nine
- Eastward Journey

"It is not the destination where you end up but the mishaps and memories you create along the way."
—Penelope Riley

Ellie had become an expert in packing the car and performing the logistical requirements for traveling across the country. She returned to the East Coast to complete a nine-month course, further enhancing her knowledge of military subjects and developing the skills necessary to compete for leadership and staff positions. She returned to the East Coast using the same route she had taken for the California-bound journey. Her father had passed away during the time she spent in San Francisco, and she wanted to visit with her mother for a short while.

She felt confident in her driving skills, but still recalled the incident of the car that followed her in Southern California. Comfortable but cautious, luck remained with Ellie as she drove east. The journey occurred in late November, and meteorologists predicted an early snowstorm for northern Arizona and New Mexico; however, she planned her start time to get ahead of the storm. Late one afternoon, the storm caught up with her just west of Albuquerque. Snow was falling faster and beginning to collect on the road. Daylight was fading. Anxious to get off the road immediately, she found a hotel outside of Albuquerque and took the last available room. She unloaded a few belongings from Lady Blue and deposited them in the room. Then, she had a quick dinner at a nearby restaurant within walking distance. She wondered if she could get Lady Blue through the snow in the morning, as the snow came down extremely hard.

After settling in for the night, she heard a knock on the door. Upon opening the door, Ellie saw the hotel manager, a young couple in their thirties, and two small children. The couple asked her if she would let the children stay in her room for the night, while they slept in their sleeping bags in the car. She looked around and deduced that they could all fit snugly in the room. She invited the entire family to stay in her room that night. The couple offered to pay for half the room, but Ellie declined. This incident was the first time Ellie felt that she had genuinely helped her fellow man in time of need; she slept well.

The roads had been closed the night before, but the snow had quit falling. Ellie and her roommates went to the restaurant to eat breakfast, determine the eastbound road conditions on the interstate, and learn when they could leave. At noon, the parties discovered the interstate was open and cleared for eastbound traffic. She reflected on the experience from the previous night as she drove down the road, realizing she had lost half a day of driving. Ellie still maintained a peaceful, joyful feeling about sharing her dwelling with strangers who needed a place to stay. The snowstorm did not faze Lady Blue.

To help with Ellie's driving time, Lee and the family met her at their mother's house for a mini-reunion. Their mother had lost a lot of weight and did not eat much; Ellie sensed her mental and emotional state was beginning to decline due to her isolation. The second evening after dinner, as the group watched television, Ellie looked over and saw that her mother's head had dropped to her chest. When Ellie shook her mother's shoulder and spoke to her to awaken her, their mother slurred her speech. Ellie's trip was delayed by two additional days while her mother was in the hospital. Her mother had experienced a minor stroke, but her cognition was good, and her speech improved.

Ellie and Lee had their first serious discussion: what would they do about their mother? They finally decided their mother could no longer live alone, so she should live with one of them. According to societal expectations, Ellie, the oldest, should take care of their mother. Living with Ellie would not be a good idea. Her career demanded relocation to different assignments every three years or so. And Ellie had worked so hard and come so far; she did not want to leave the military and take care of her mother. She asked Lee if he would agree to take care of their mother. He had a stable life and was married with kids; he and his family could care for her. Lee agreed. Ellie presented two options to her mother without an accompanying rationale for each. "We have decided that it is best you no longer live alone. Do you want to live with me or Lee?" "Lee," she responded. Ellie simultaneously felt relieved and rejected. Their mother enjoyed many more years living close to Lee and the grandkids. Maybe their mother understood the situation better than Ellie and made the best decision for all concerned.

In a couple of days, she was back on the road and had no time to waste, as she had lost a few days attending to her mother's health situation. Luck remained with her, and she encountered no obstacles to the progress of her journey. As she drove through the main gate of the installation where she had her first basic training course, a warm feeling passed over her, like seeing an old friend. Unlike the first brief time she resided here, Ellie was assigned to older quarters, sharing a kitchen with a male neighbor. Not satisfied with this arrangement, she soon obtained off-post housing with two of her classmates, one male and one female. The dwelling with three bedrooms and three bathrooms was a sizeable duplex in a neighboring town. They all thought this would meet their expectations of not needing supervision; after all, they had proven they could handle what the military and life had thrown their way. However, this house paled compared to the bay-front apartment in California she left behind. There would never be another like it.

The personalities of the 70-plus classmates merged into one, exhibiting both positive and negative attributes of any one of the individuals. The faculty feared them, and they became very close. Collectively, they brought military experience from field and staff units, complementing each other. They questioned statements made by the faculty, inquired about the source of data presented, and suggested alternative perspectives on the situations. The class theme song was "Another One Bites the Dust" by Queen. The faculty played this song as a tribute to the class when they received their diplomas upon graduation. Faculty and students had to work to earn each other's respect. Ellie made good friendships; unfortunately, through time, friends leave our thoughts for more extended periods, stretching into years. Friendships formed during military assignments proved difficult to maintain. She learned to transform sadness or loneliness into thoughts of embracing the present.

Ellie saw much more of the Maryland landscape this time with Lady Blue. There were weekend trips to New York and Pennsylvania, trips to military air bases to drop off friends on their way to new assignments, trips to the Maryland shore, and drives to parties. Whenever possible, Ellie would catch a ride with other friends, one of whom was the designated driver. If she drove solo, Ellie limited her drinks to one. There was no tolerance for DUIs or drugs in the military; it was a career killer.

Chapter Ten
- California Bound Again

"Monterey is a place, a grating noise, a quality of light, a tone, a habit, a nostalgia, a dream."
— John Steinbeck

Time passed quickly, and soon, the class prepared to move on to their new assignment. Ellie requested orders for Germany and was surprised to learn she would return to California, less than a year after she left. She knew there was a good reason for this and looked forward to the new assignment in the Monterrey area. The seafood was rated some of the best in the country, and Monterey Bay would provide a peaceful place to restore her soul and replenish her energy after a long 60-hour workweek.

The return trip to California would be via Interstate 80, as it presented another opportunity to see part of the country she had never seen. Additionally, Ellie would have a traveling companion. One of her classmates was using the route to go to Washington state. She would drive behind her and go south when she reached California. It was reassuring to know someone she trusted would be close by if there was trouble on the road. She had a mechanic thoroughly check Lady Blue before the long trip; she was ready for another long journey to fine-tune the engine. The most memorable scenery was on the last part of the route—the Great Salt Lake Flats of Utah. What a phenomenal place, considering that 11,000 years ago, it was a lake. Approximately 35 miles wide and occupying an area of around 4,000 square miles, the Salt Lake Desert must be seen to be appreciated. It had been the loneliest stretch of road Ellie had experienced so far. She was glad when she reached the western side of the desert, which was beautiful in its unique way. In three days, the travel team had reached California; Ellie said goodbye, promising to keep in touch, knowing that the commitment would fade with time.

Ellie headed south to Monterey and looked forward to the beautiful scenery along the coast. She was grateful for the incident-free driving and finding lodging when she stopped for the night. Lady Blue was enjoying herself. Many years later, when Ellie reflected on her cross-country trips, she pondered the source of peace and calm on the drive; what happened to that peace as she got older? She stopped in San Francisco to visit the last boyfriend in whom she had invested so much of herself. She perceived him differently now, and although the pain had not completely healed, Ellie knew the relationship was finally over. He called her a few times after she moved to Monterey. The last time he called, she told him she was seeing someone else and no longer wanted to maintain contact with him. It was over.

Driving south on Highway 1 along the coast, she looked forward to her new assignment. Admiring the scenery, she felt peaceful and was positive that she was still traveling the path intended for her. Not far from the Monterey city limit sign, she saw a sign for the installation where she would work for the next three years. Front gate security personnel provided directions to the unit headquarters, where she would be assigned. She had no idea how beautiful the location would be. It was on Monterey Bay. She made many unit runs to the officers' club built on a small peninsula jutting into the bay. Ellie could see the water when she stepped out of the building where she worked.

Although the Army had appointed a sponsor to assist Ellie with settling into her new assignment, she found her way around independently, having survived the system for almost five years. Apartment hunting had become a frustrating experience since housing was costly in the city, and she could not find a place by the water. Several people suggested she try the neighboring town of Salinas; it was a short drive, and the cost of rental property was lower.

Salinas was twenty minutes inland from where she worked. Lettuce fields dotted the landscape on her commuting route between home and work. Although not located near the water, she found a new home in a very nice, modern apartment in Salinas with a lovely balcony overlooking the agricultural fields that provided food to the rest of the country. It was an easy, relaxing commute each day. Lady Blue could have driven the route without any interjection from Ellie. She experienced a slight mishap while driving through the lettuce field after working late one night. The right rear tire on Lady Blue blew out, forcing Ellie to drive into one of the lettuce fields near her home. She managed to get the car out of the field and drive about 10 minutes with the bad tire to a service station, where they replaced the flat tire with the spare. She bought a new tire the next day. Someone broke into Lady Blue and stole the stereo system the following night. Ellie always thought someone who worked at the service station did it because they retrieved her address when she paid. She thought it was too coincidental. Between the new tire and a new stereo system for Lady Blue, she didn't have much money for the rest of the month.

This assignment was more demanding physically and mentally, but Ellie possessed the stamina to weather the rough spots. She devoted many off-duty hours to the gym, developing her upper body strength and running to build endurance. She was performing the skills that the Army had trained her to do. It was the next crucial stage in officer development, and Ellie wanted to succeed as she always had.

She had some dates with men assigned to the installation. However, she did not need to be part of a couple, as it was not a priority with Ellie. She was developing herself with all the faults and accomplishments associated with living. After a few weeks, she met another officer in another unit. They became friends and even worked on the same project together. They appreciated each other for their work ethic and competence; as far as Ellie was concerned, he was the best friend she had at that time. On one particular Friday, when all the work she performed during the day was of poor quality, and nothing seemed to be going right, she left her desk to speak with her supervisor. While she was away, her best friend left a yellow Post-it note with a smiley face drawn on it. He did not sign his name on it, but Ellie knew it was from him. They went to happy hour after work that day and talked for hours. While she cherished the friendship, she did not want the friendship to change to a romantic relationship, as she had no plans to remarry.

But it did change. One Friday night after happy hour, he stayed overnight at her place. She felt it was prudent to do this since they both had exceeded their alcohol limit. He slept on the couch downstairs, and she slept in her bed upstairs. The next morning, Ellie, out of apprehension of an uncomfortable situation, informed the young man that she thought it would be best if they did not see each other anymore. He walked out on the apartment balcony and stood for a few minutes. Ellie approached him and inquired how he was feeling. Eyes moist, he told her he did not want to go; he wanted to be with her. Ellie's compassionate nature always prevailed; she took his hand and asked him if he would like to walk through Carmel. One stop on that excursion was an ice cream shop. Walking down the sidewalk of Carmel with ice cream cones in hand, they enjoyed each other's company. Suddenly, just as he was about to take a lick off his ice cream, the double-dipper fell onto the sidewalk. They both laughed heartily, and Ellie shared her cone with him.

While she was adjusting to a new relationship, she received word from home that her sister had passed away after a two-year battle with colon cancer. Ellie and her sister were not that close primarily due to a seven-year age difference; as Ellie was approaching her early teenage years, her sister was in her late teens. They shared a bedroom for a while, respecting each other and pursuing their rights to space and quietness when needed. Ellie remembered the night her sister married. Their favorite aunt, who came in for the wedding, slept in the bed with Ellie. Nestled in bed, Ellie started crying, explaining to her aunt, "I miss her." Growing up in a family that never expressed those terms of endearment to each other, missing her sister was the closest she had come to expressing love for her older sister. Realizing she would never see her sister again was hard to accept. Her friend and companion remarked that he would like to accompany her home for the funeral. Although Ellie would have liked the company and support, she felt it was not the proper time to meet the family. She thanked him for his offer, explaining it was something she needed to do alone.

A few months later, Ellie and her beau went snow skiing at Lake Tahoe. During the second evening, after they had enjoyed a wonderful dinner, he presented her with a ruby ring and a marriage proposal. She was surprised at this since she had indicated to him on more than one occasion that she did not want to remarry. She refused the ring and the marriage proposal, feeling frustrated with his actions and guilty for rejecting his intentions. He responded by saying he wanted her to keep the ring anyway. She asked him to leave her alone for a while. Ellie wrestled with her thoughts and emotions for the next couple of hours. Her male supervisors had told her that it would be a good idea if she got married, complying with societal expectations. She appreciated and respected him and loved his company, but the type of love required for a successful marriage did not exist.

Later that evening, she approached him in another room to render her final position. Ellie told him she was unsure if she could remarry and was uncertain about her feelings for him. She suggested they live together for a year, after which time they would decide how to move forward. He had never married and had no firsthand knowledge of the compromise required between partners in a marriage. However, during their time together, he had learned that considering a partner's opinion was extremely important. He had helped Ellie through a grieving period when her sister passed away. Ellie realized she possessed the type of love required for a successful marriage. She also understood that the military was no longer an experiment; she was now committed to working hard to achieve whatever success the military offered to her. The military gave her a sense of being part of an entity with a higher purpose than her selfish motives. She was proud to wear the uniform, serve her country, and work alongside like-minded individuals, knowing she was making a difference in the world.

Three months after the one-year deadline, on January 2nd, Ellie married Lundy, whose name means "a new beginning." And it was a new beginning for both, especially Ellie. There was a holiness to their relationship, another life-altering event for her. They became life partners, intimately aware of their career challenges, deployments, military politics, lengthy separations due to assignment changes, the importance of supporting each other's career advancements, and sharing household tasks. They both loved to travel and explore. Their assignments provided many opportunities for travel—temporary duty in various locations, volksmarching in Germany, visits to neighboring countries, opportunities to experience stateside travel, and local assignment locations.

Chapter Eleven
- Germany Bound

"Germany has become a country that many people abroad associate with hope."
—Angela Merkel

The first year of their marriage was the first test of their solid relationship. Ellie and Lundy were unit commanders, which was challenging, but adding to their obstacles, their units were 70 miles apart. One primary responsibility was to remain readily available to handle emergencies that may arise within the unit. They only saw each other on weekends. However, they managed to take a one-week vacation to celebrate their honeymoon in San Diego, as they could not do so after the wedding due to work obligations the next day. San Diego was their first real trip as a married couple. It was another opportunity to focus on being together in new settings. It was fun, the food was great, and they had an exciting sailing adventure. After making a mid-week reservation, they embarked on a schooner to sail San Diego Bay for a few hours. The boat was beautiful, and the scenery gorgeous. On the way back into port, the sky grew dark, and the wind increased as a sudden storm approached. The small but competent crew immediately began adjusting the sails. All the passengers were ordered into the mess to ride out the storm. Within minutes, the boat pitched in all directions; the storm tossed the mess area below the water level. All were concerned that they would not survive this. Forty-five minutes later, the boat settled down, and the wind was calm. Breaks in the clouds revealed a beautiful sunset forming.

Two and a half years later, Ellie and Lundy were still together and planning tasks in preparation for their next assignment. They had both received orders for Germany. She was anxious to go, as she had never been to a foreign country, much less lived or worked in one. Lundy would become her guide since he was stationed there several years earlier. The only obstacle was that Lundy had to report to Germany three months earlier than she did. She considered this in her favor as he would arrive earlier and have their living quarters set up when she joined him. He shipped his car to Germany. The last three months in Monterey were hectic. Relinquishing command left an emptiness in her heart. She had devoted two years to leading soldiers, providing logistics support to combat units, and developing military skills to increase her opportunities for future promotions. Before she left California, the military selected her for a promotion.

Her plan for getting to Germany was not a streamlined one. She had to find a home for Lady Blue because she did not want to take her to Germany, as she would likely have difficulty getting repairs done if needed. Ellie decided to leave her car with her brother in Arkansas; he was a good sport about babysitting a cheap Japanese-made car. She would worry from time to time because there were no dealerships in the area where he lived to perform repairs if needed. She reconciled herself to the fact that this was still the best decision and left Lady Blue's future in the hands of her brother.

Ellie was also tired of traversing the country by herself. She asked her sister-in-law, Sue, if she would like to accompany her during her drive from California to Arkansas. Her response was an enthusiastic "Yes." It was an opportunity for her to fly for the first time, see California, and take a break from the kids for a while. Ellie had shipped all her belongings to storage for later movement to Germany. She was living in a hotel when her sister-in-law flew into San Francisco. Ellie picked her up at the airport, and they drove to Monterey to stay the night. Ellie treated Sue to a nice dinner in a restaurant that had once been a church. The food was delicious, and Ellie knew Sue enjoyed it. This meal was the first time Sue had tasted fish other than fried catfish or tuna in a can. This was also the first time she had consumed an alcoholic drink—a white wine recommended by Ellie, who had acquired her knowledge of wines from Lundy, who had taken a sommelier course in a community college. She was impressed with his expertise, and they enjoyed many bottles of wine during their meals, sometimes even two bottles. He always said that, for the price, California wines were the best.

Sue did not know how to drive a stick shift, so she couldn't help Ellie drive Lady Blue. She stayed busy looking at all the sights, especially in the cities as they passed through. When they arrived in Arizona, they took a detour to see the Grand Canyon, rated as the eighth-largest in size globally. Neither of them had seen this canyon. It was a wondrous sight, challenging their imaginations regarding its formation through the centuries. They experienced no adverse events during the trip, but Ellie knew Sue was anxious to get home and see the kids. Ellie rested for two days, then flew from Oklahoma City to Frankfurt, Germany, making connecting flights en route.

Chapter Twelve
- Adjusting to Life in Germany

"Was mich nicht umbringt, macht mich stärker."
("What does not kill me will make me stronger.")
— German Cliche

When Ellie entered the baggage claim area at Frankfurt International Airport, she battled contradictory emotions of excitement and fear of being in a foreign environment. Having never flown on an international flight, Ellie was intimidated by the customs process. Luckily, the German agent who processed her through the queue spoke fluent English. Then, she finally met Lundy after exiting customs. Ellie was thrilled to see him and anxious to leave the airport. They drove to their new home, a split-level apartment within walking distance of Ellie's job and a short drive to Lundy's. It was newly constructed, spacious, and had a lovely rear balcony view of a flower garden. Back then, German houses were built without closets to avoid paying taxes, as closets were considered rooms in Germany. This situation prompted the purchase of shrunks (large chests of drawers in the United States) for hanging clothes. The kitchen cabinets were minimal, but a washer and dryer were outside the kitchen. It would be fun and frustrating adjusting to living the German way, which she much preferred to living in government quarters.

The apartment was in a row of similar apartments, each with its own parking space in a community parking lot at the front of the buildings. None of the neighbors spoke English. Although Ellie studied German for two years in college, she was not proficient enough in German to converse with any of them. The landlord and his wife spoke very little English. They came by the apartment a few weeks after Ellie and Lundy had settled in to see how things were going. The conversations were slow and awkward at times, but they all managed to convey key points to each other. When Lundy presented the landlord with a bottle of Scotch as a gift, they became friends for life. Living in the apartment was a pleasant experience. The only complaint neighbors had with the American couple, as communicated to the landlord, was that there was too much noise when Lundy started the car early each morning to go to work. Lundy parked the vehicle at the end of the parking lot, hoping to alleviate the noise. It worked because there were no more complaints. They were down to one car now, as there was no need for two, given the proximity of their workplaces. Ellie walked to work every day, even in the snow.

Their jobs were extremely demanding and essential to the Army's mission in Germany. Since this was Lundy's second tour in Germany, he could relax and do his job without external distractions. Ellie, on the other hand, not only had to work very hard at her job but also had to adjust to living in a foreign country. A few weeks after her arrival, she woke up one morning with nausea, chills, and a fever; evidently, her immune system reacted to strange viruses or bacteria in her environment. For the first time, she had to rely on someone else to call her workplace and let them know she was sick. Within two days, she was strong enough to return to work.

After a few months, life settled down, and they began to see the country. On rare weekends when there was time, they would go on Volk marches. These are 10-kilometer or 20-kilometer walks in various locations throughout the country. They usually walked the 10-kilometer walk and ended each by rewarding themselves with a beer and kasebrot (cheese bread) in the fest tent. On one march in Strasbourg, France, they enjoyed beer and pommes frites (french fries). These marches provided the perfect opportunity to see the country and interact with the locals.

Proximity to other countries enabled Ellie and Lundy to explore outside Germany on long holiday weekends and rare vacations. They traveled to England, Scotland, France, Austria, East Berlin (still controlled by the USSR then), Belgium, the Netherlands, and Switzerland. They treasured the moments they could travel because both spent so much time participating in field maneuvers that were essential to the mission.

Midway through their tour, the military reassigned them to new units; however, their units were not stationed near each other this time. They moved to a smaller town north of Frankfurt, close to Ellie's workplace. Lundy would commute approximately 45 minutes each way to his work every day. This arrangement necessitated the purchase of a second car. They decided to buy a new BMW American specification sedan, thinking they would retire Lundy's car at the end of their assignment. Ellie drove the new car, and Lundy continued to drive his older Volkswagen Sirocco. She often thought of Lady Blue.

Their jobs were extremely demanding in many aspects—time, distance, responsibility, numerous field deployments, and absences from each other. Ellie and Lundy successfully planned and executed a general inspection of their unit plans and operations. The results of the inspection, conducted by higher headquarters, could make or break a career. A year and a half passed quickly. Ellie received orders to report to another military course back home, another rung up on the ladder. Lundy received orders to report stateside three months after Ellie.

Chapter Thirteen
- Good to be Home
-Sight Loss Event 2

"Home is any four walls that enclose the right person."
—Helen Rowland

The course was in Virginia. Ellie had driven through Virginia a few times, always enjoying the beautiful scenery but displeased with the traffic on Interstate 95. Looking forward to returning to the United States, she reflected upon her years in Germany. While it was educational, exposing her to many different cultures, governments, and indescribable beauty, she realized the truthfulness of the emotional joy of returning to one's native country with all its good points and bad points. European immigrants founded the United States of America, whose varied influences are evident in the country's cities and small towns. Ellie felt blessed with the opportunity to see and participate in so many foreign experiences. Her Germany tour of duty aroused a lasting travel spirit within her; she longed to see more of the world.

Ellie was curious to see how this joint-service course would proceed. Having attended only Army courses in the past, now her classmates would come from all the services. The class instructor was a Marine; the assistant class instructor was from the Army. Her assigned seat was between a Navy Lieutenant Commander and an Air Force fighter pilot. Ellie was a member of "Class Six," consisting of twenty military officers; appropriately, the class members designated the class name as the six-shooters. The class softball team was named Class Act to illustrate a warm acceptance of the two females in the class. All class members contributed somehow to their success as the season's first-place winners. Class instruction centered on team building and demonstrating the criticality of considering different points of view in military planning and operations. Each service brought its perspective, which contributed to the overarching strategy.

The most valuable memory from the educational experience was a comment made by the Navy Lieutenant Commander who sat next to her. One class session was devoted to an issue that each student presented for discussion. Ellie chose the subject of reverse discrimination by comparing how the military selected males and females for the course. She explained that she was fully cognizant that a male officer was denied attendance to the course, which allowed her admission. While she was grateful for the opportunity to attend the elite course, she was humbled by a perceived sacrifice made to enable her selection. After the session, the Naval officer approached her and told her he would fight beside her any day. She would never forget that moment.

Midway through the course, Lundy returned to the

States. He spent two weeks with Ellie before reporting to his assignment in northern Virginia. From then on until the end of the course, they saw each other on weekends. Lundy spent his free time searching for a house to purchase, their first as a couple. After Ellie graduated from the course, they took three weeks off to fly to Arkansas to pick up Lady Blue, drive her to Virginia, buy a house in the Mount Vernon area near a metro station, and move their household goods into their new home.

Ellie's new orders required her to report to a newly created command that served as the Army component to a Joint command. The command's mission was research and development of space-based strategic and tactical missile defense and other technologies. She had to retrain her brain from combat unit logistics to research involving unknown technology. Her travel lust was partially satisfied by traveling to foreign countries to work with allies on their technology. This assignment was probably her most interesting.

It was during this assignment that "Sight Loss Event 2" occurred. During a routine annual eye exam, Ellie received a report indicating she no longer had 20/20 vision, unlike previous ones. She had noticed that reading had become a little more difficult, but at 41 years old, she asked herself, "Vision changes as we age, doesn't it?" After all, her mother had worn glasses most of her life. The optometrist conducting the exam informed Ellie that she had a bad case of macular drusen in the retina of each eye and said, "You are going to have a lot of trouble with your vision in the future." He explained that drusen are yellow deposits of lipids and proteins under the retina. The retina converts light that enters the eye into electrical signals, which the optic nerve transmits to the brain, creating the images one sees. Ellie knew nothing about this ailment and did not want to know at this point in her life. But her vision was no longer 20/20, so she received a prescription for reading glasses. She placed this incident in a secluded place inside her mind and forgot about it for a while. She bought prescription glasses and continued with her busy life.

After years had passed and internet searches became prevalent, Ellie discovered that the deposits can vary in size. Small ones are common in people 50 and older who do not have age-related macular degeneration (AMD). If a person has many small or large drusen, they often exhibit signs of AMD. AMD affects central vision, decreasing the ability to see fine details. The macula, a part of the retina, is damaged. Ellie could eventually lose the ability to drive, see faces, and read small print; she may even need help performing everyday activities. Since AMD is a degenerative retinal disease, Ellie realized the seriousness of the situation. She never knew that the retina of the eyes is so vital. She began to take vitamins recommended for people who have been diagnosed with AMD. Prescription eyeglasses readily alleviated Ellie's vision issues for many years. There is no cure for AMD; it is a hereditary disease. Overwhelmed, she added this information to that hidden place in her mind.

Chapter Fourteen - **Lady Blue Era Ends**

"It has been one hell of a ride."
—Anonymous

Ellie unpacked all the moving boxes, placed the furniture in selected spaces, and the household items in new positions. She reported to her research and development job two days later. The weather report for the first day she reported to work was foreboding—the meteorologist predicted a snowstorm would bring approximately two feet of snow. She took the metro to work, leaving the car in the parking lot. Mid-morning, she walked up the street to attend a meeting. So far, the snow was holding off, but the wind had picked up a bit, and the sky was gray. The early afternoon brought the first snow, which began to freeze on contact and accumulate on the street. Everyone in the office decided it would be wise to head home early. Ellie wanted to finish a small project before she headed out. Before she knew it, it was dark outside, and she and her boss were the only two people left in the office.

They both decided to leave immediately. Ellie headed toward the metro station. Officials at the metro informed everyone trying to leave the city that the metro had closed all the stations. Still calm, she headed to the hotel across the street from her work location. Snow accumulation was approaching one foot. People crowded in the hotel lobby in the same situation as her. Planning to get a room for the night, a patient, pleasant desk clerk informed her that there were no more rooms. Most people in the lobby stayed there overnight. She went to the public phone booth (cell phones did not exist at the time) to call Lundy and tell him her situation. When he responded that he would drive to get her, she told him the roads were impassable and snow was still coming down hard. She told him she would remain in the hotel lobby overnight and touch base with him in the morning. Around 10:00 PM, Ellie saw Lundy enter the hotel lobby. How did he manage this? He collected her belongings and told Ellie to follow him.

Their friend Adam was outside the hotel's front door, driving his large Volvo wagon; it had enough clearance to navigate the road. Ellie and Lundy jumped into the car and slowly made their way home. Lundy didn't drive their car because he could not get it out of the driveway. He walked half a mile to Adam's house to get help, or maybe he just wanted a friend to lean on. Adam said he thought he could drive the ten miles up the Washington Parkway. It took them an hour, but they managed to make it. Now, the three of them had to drive back home. Within an hour, Ellie and Lundy had returned to their newly purchased home, where snow was still falling. What a way to spend a first day at work.

Government offices were closed the next day because of the snow accumulation. Ellie and Lundy took turns shoveling snow from the fifty-foot driveway in front of their house. In a short time, a city snowplow covered the entrance with more snow as it cleared the street. They shoveled snow many more times while living in Virginia.

After a year of owning a home, Lundy and Ellie discovered the house owned them. Mortgage, insurance, maintenance, upgrades, lawn maintenance, utility payments, shoveling snow from the driveway, and countless other tasks were taken in stride, leaving them with less time for having fun. They reaffirmed a commitment to turn the house into an investment that would generate a profit when they sold it.

Many local attractions offered short day or weekend trips near their residence. Because they were both Civil War enthusiasts, Ellie and Lundy went to all the Civil War battlefields in and around northern Virginia. They left each site with heavy hearts because so many lost their lives during this conflict: brother against brother, father against son, and so on. The Battle of Antietam in Pennsylvania, known as the war's bloodiest battle, particularly moved Ellie. Documentation indicates that blood filled the ditches. Trips to Savannah and Charleston rendered a longing for the genteel culture of the South in the nineteenth century. Key West was a highlight as they both loved the ocean and beach. Key West, the southernmost point in the country, presented a beautiful camera shot for Lundy. He always had his camera and an assortment of lenses with him. A sailboat sailed across the water backlit by the sun; he had to capture it. Click! Done. After the boat disappeared, Lundy noticed he had not removed the lens cover. This time was well before smartphones existed. There were numerous visits to various sites in Washington, D.C., including the Vietnam Veterans Memorial, the Smithsonian Museum, the White House, the Lincoln Memorial, and the Washington Monument.

Because of her work, Ellie traveled solo to European countries and the Middle East for conferences regarding technology projects of mutual interest to the governments of those countries and the United States. On a couple of occasions, Lundy met her after business ended. Then they spent a few days traveling in those locations with diplomatic passports. They were very blessed to be able to participate in extraordinary educational and leisure journeys that most people could never imagine.

About three years into the tour, Ellie and Lundy decided to go to Jamaica. They needed a beach break and had never traveled to a developing Caribbean country. The pictures in the travel brochure were very enticing. They tempered their sense of adventure and wisely decided to stay the week in a gated resort. They rented a car at the airport, planning to travel around the island. Lundy drove since motorists drive on the left side of the road, as in Great Britain. They were surprised when they picked up the rental car at the small airport. It was an old, beat-up, noisy piece of junk. They hoped it would not break down on the trip, since no AAA service was available there. They ventured out on the first day to walk down the street to a local grocery store to buy snacks. No larger than a 7-Eleven, the shelves were mostly empty. They managed to buy some Pringles chips to accompany the Red Stripe beer, which they would consume during happy hour before dinner. One excursion to Ocho Rios produced an incident with a Rastafarian who demanded money after Lundy took his picture. Lundy gave him some money after a futile one-sided conversation with the citizen. Lundy never had that photo developed. Rundown shacks strewn along the poorly maintained road served as homes for many people. It was an interesting time, but it would always be their least favorite trip.

On the first Monday after the trip, Ellie's boss greeted and instructed her to report to the "big" boss. Nervous about the purpose of this request, she mentally weighed several options. He asked her to sit down; her heart dropped. Rather than the bad news she had expected, he congratulated her on being selected as a battalion commander in Germany, the first female support battalion commander in the corps where she would be assigned. Ellie could not believe it; what an honor and tremendous responsibility. She would report in six months.

Within those six months, Ellie and Lundy sold the house (at a sizable profit), sold the BMW, and bought a new car to ship to Germany. A couple of years prior, Lundy had sold the Sirocco and bought a Subaru wagon; as homeowners, they needed a vehicle that they could use to haul things. They shipped both new cars to Germany. Now, they had to decide what to do with Lady Blue. She was 14 years old, and although she was still in top shape, they both felt that it would not be right to leave her with someone who may have to confront serious maintenance issues. Ellie loved that car. She and Lady Blue had been through so many good times, and the thought of not having that car in her life left a profound emptiness, as if her identity would disappear. One day, she told Lundy they needed to find a new owner; it was time to let Lady Blue go. Lundy placed an ad in the newspaper; eBay was still a figment of someone's imagination when this occurred. Several people expressed an interest. They decided to sell Lady Blue to a pleasant young man who wanted a 280Z. He came by late one day. He took her for a spin, wrote a check, and drove Lady Blue away. Ellie cried herself to sleep that night.

Part II: Difficult Times Ahead

Chapter Fifteen
- Life Partners

"It was the best of times, it was the worst of times, it was the age of wisdom, it was the age of foolishness, it was the epoch of belief, it was the epoch of incredulity, it was the season of light, it was the season of darkness, it was the spring of hope, it was the winter of despair."
— Charles Dickens

Fall weather with pleasant days and cool nights greeted Ellie and Lundy when they arrived in Germany, the second time for her and the third time for him. They had never changed duty stations at the same time. From Frankfurt airport, they took the train to Nuremberg. Ellie's soon-to-be executive officer met them there and transported them to their final destination, a small Bavarian village adjacent to a tank training area. Before the Americans took control of it after World War II, it was a German tank training area in rustic, beautiful Bavaria. Unlike life in the cosmopolitan Frankfurt area during their first tour in Germany, they would spend the next couple of years in the boonies, with the closest city of any size being Nuremberg. But then again, city life was of no concern since Ellie knew she would spend most of her time in the field on various maneuvers and training events.

They were driven to temporary lodging for a few weeks until their household goods and cars reached Germany. The accommodation was very comfortable and contained all the necessities to get through a temporary situation. When they opened the door to the quarters, a welcome basket containing an assortment of German snacks and pastries greeted them. The basket was a kind gesture from the unit and was much appreciated. They were too exhausted to eat anything and went to bed early because they had to be up early to return to Nuremberg the next morning. There they would meet Ellie's new boss, who would present her with a promotion to the next rank in a small ceremony including the three of them and the adjutant who read the orders. Since Lundy had served with him several years prior, Lundy would help promote a good relationship with her new boss.

While Ellie was waiting to assume command in two days, she completed the items required of any military person reporting to a new assignment. Lundy, likewise, was busy reporting to his new position as the Deputy Installation Commander. The two of them were a novelty.

Typically, a male officer would command the unit for which Ellie would soon be responsible; Lundy became the leader of the officers' wives' organization, a role usually performed by the wife of the male commander. All people living and working at the small installation were intrigued to see how this situation would develop. One of Lundy's co-workers loaned them a car to use until their cars arrived at Bremerhaven.

The weather for the change of command was pleasant, with cloudy skies and no precipitation. The ceremony was going smoothly. The battalion flag changed hands, and Ellie gave her remarks as the incoming commander; next up was the outgoing commander's speech. Just as he began his remarks, the public address system went silent. He gave his speech anyway, but most people could not hear it. During the reception, the executive officer told Ellie that a soldier who did not hold the outgoing commander in high regard had turned the system off. The company commander later dealt with this young man. It was an interesting start to the first day of a 26-month assignment. There would be many more interesting days.

Within a few weeks, Lundy and a coworker drove to Bremerhaven to pick up the cars. Soon, the movers delivered the household goods to the designated commanders' quarters. Lundy and Ellie called it the bowling alley. Located on the second floor, they had to climb stairs to reach it. There was a long hallway that extended the entire length of the building with rooms on either side. At one end was the living area, dining area, and kitchen. It was not the architectural layout that they preferred, but they would not be there for long, as brand-new quarters would soon be available. They resided there for just a few months. Then they moved into the new house designated for commanders. The second set of quarters was a duplex, which they shared with one of the other battalion commanders and his family. It was lovely and built to suit American home construction tastes. They resided in the third living quarters for approximately nine months. It was large and well-suited for hosting their numerous social events. Three moves in two years added an extra burden to the already challenging command environment that Ellie and Lundy faced.

Just as Ellie settled into a comfortable stride addressing her responsibilities, the military notified her and many other unit commanders that they would be deploying to Iraq to support Operation Desert Storm. Suddenly, the mission priorities shifted to preparing the unit for deployment. Personnel and equipment had to be ready for sea and/or air movement. Amazingly, unit morale was exceedingly high; all felt a sense of purpose for the training they had received in past years. Ellie and the other unit personnel tested the training and experience that they had accumulated. Lundy also volunteered for deployment; he knew this was what he had prepared for. Once in the country, they would probably not see or communicate with each other for a very long time. She put these thoughts in a secluded place in her mind. Preparing for war was the all-consuming focus.

Within two months, the orders changed. The military informed Ellie, Lundy, and several units that they would not be deploying after all. They focused all mission support efforts on preparing the deploying units for a conflict in the desert. The units that did not deploy provided personnel and equipment to the deploying units to bring them up to 100 percent operability. Military equipment had to be repaired and prepared for shipment. The deploying personnel had to attend to their family affairs, get their personal equipment in order, comply with medical directives, and spend as much time as possible with their families. After three months, Ellie's unit was down to 60 percent authorized personnel and 75 percent authorized equipment. The non-deploying units became nearly inoperable. After the deploying units left, Ellie had just one thought: How would her unit support the units for which she was responsible?

For six months, all the units that did not deploy pulled together to continue training and sustaining equipment, the most challenging task, as repair parts usually shipped from stateside were diverted to the theater of operations. Lundy was very busy as the Officers' Wives Group leader, helping them with issues related to enlisted families. During the conflict, Army leadership made decisions that affected the structure of the Army. Units were inactivated, resized, or realigned. These changes became effective upon redeployment of forces from the theater of operations. The division to which Ellie's unit was assigned did not return to Germany; it went back to the States. Ellie's battalion and the brigade she supported were attached to another division; the name of her unit changed. The rest of her command consisted of rebuilding what she could and changing processes and procedures to accommodate new leadership. But she and Lundy survived; they had become life partners tested as many couples can only imagine. She must have done something right, as the military extended her command duties for two months during all the turmoil. All the wives hated to see Lundy leave.

A few months before they left this assignment, Lundy failed the run portion of the physical training test. How was this possible since he ran marathons? Complaints about his hip hurting prompted Ellie to insist he see a doctor in Nuremberg. The doctor ordered him to be evacuated immediately to Walter Reed Hospital in Washington, D.C. After a week of tests and exams, the medical staff was unable to determine the cause of his hip pain and sent him back to Germany. Except for changing eye glass prescriptions, Ellie's health was good.

Chapter Sixteen
- This Can't Be Happening

"When you get to the end of your rope,
tie a knot and hang on."
—Theodore Roosevelt

Their next assignment in Germany was in Heidelberg, a premier location. They moved into four-flex military quarters, which were adequate but lacked some of the modern American features they enjoyed in their previous quarters. Both worked in major headquarters positions, which meant little or no field duty and free weekends. They explored the countryside during their free weekends. Volksmarching on weekends was a favorite pastime. Still lurking in their minds was Lundy's physical dilemma. After a few weeks, Lundy received a call from Walter Reed Hospital ordering him to report to the States for consultation. Had Ellie known that the diagnosis revelation would shock the foundation of their relationship, she would have returned with him. A young female Army Major interning at Walter Reed had determined the source of Lundy's hip pain. Examination of a urine sample retrieved during his last visit revealed the presence of a particular protein indicative of multiple myeloma, a bone marrow disease. This disease was a terminal diagnosis; doctors informed him his life expectancy was five years.

A week after Lundy left Germany to go to Walter Reed, he called Ellie to tell her he would be home in two days. Upon returning from the trip, he asked her to sit down; he had something to say. Ellie's heart stopped. He patiently and stoically relayed the diagnosis information to her. She could not believe what she was hearing. Their life together was a blessing to both; she could not imagine life without him. Unable to grasp the situation, Ellie's ego prompted her to feel selfishly sorry for herself because she had only a finite amount of time left to spend with Lundy. She could not comprehend the pain and physical deterioration that awaited Lundy or how much he would lean on her for physical and emotional strength. She tried to hide this information in the secluded area of her mind, but to no avail. She had to make some difficult decisions. Walter Reed staff wanted Lundy to return to the States to begin working on bone marrow transplant options with the National Institute of Health (NIH). A different doctor would take over his case and provide medical care for the next three years. Ellie explained the situation to her superior, who graciously initiated arrangements for them to evacuate immediately back to the States. Lundy would report to the medical holding company at Walter Reed. The military informed Ellie of her next assignment upon her return to the States.

They spent the next week preparing to ship their cars and household goods back home. They also arranged to store their household goods until they could find a place to live. Within two weeks, they had cleared quarters in Heidelberg and processed out of their assignments in Germany. Lundy and Ellie were overwhelmed with the anticipation of their future, but they never discussed their feelings of inadequacy with each other. They kept putting one foot in front of the other, knowing they had to proceed on the path that awaited them. Although neither of them was religious, their faith in God was solid. Lundy never elaborated on the spiritual aspect of what was happening; Ellie instinctively knew that everything happened for the common good, which she may never know. But they both were too busy now to confide such feelings to each other; each had to be strong for the other. Lundy emphasized that this was his disease, not hers, to which she responded, "What happens to you happens to me."

Faced with uncertainty regarding Lundy's medical protocol, they lived in a furnished apartment for a while. A rental car was their transportation until their cars arrived in Baltimore. Lundy reported to the medical holding company at Walter Reed. His doctors arranged a consultation with medical personnel at the NIH who would provide his care. He immediately liked his doctor at the Institute, and they sent donor kits to family members to determine if one of them would be a match for a bone marrow transplant. They searched the various bone marrow databases to see if there was a match. After a month of searching, they could not find a match. The next course of action was to perform an autologous bone marrow transplant, a new procedure at the time. This new procedure involved removing some of Lundy's bone marrow, treating it with chemicals and radiation, and inserting it back into his body.

During the weeks they were awaiting donor information, Lundy and Ellie retrieved their cars, bought a house, and moved in. They purchased a townhouse in a bedroom community, located near her job. The previous owners, who happened to be interior designers, had impeccably decorated the townhouse. There was a uniquely designed brick patio with interesting plants on the lowest level and a large wooden patio on the ground level. She spent as much time as she could on these patios; they proved to be areas that provided time and quiet, which brought peace to her mind. Lundy rarely went out because his immune system was barely functioning, rendering him very susceptible to infections. They were never really attached to any of the houses where they had previously lived. They both knew the dwellings were only temporary; the only quality that made them a home was the presence of Lundy and Ellie. The Army found a position for Ellie that was not too demanding. However, it was career-enhancing. Of course, both were functioning in a daze. Ellie knew she was not giving her all to her new job, but somehow, it no longer seemed that important.

Lundy never had another military assignment. The Army had planned to give him a medical discharge after 18 years of service. He was disheartened because he wanted to retire after 20 years of service. Luckily, a young man in the Walter Reed medical holding administration office used the system to enable Lundy to remain on active duty until he reached 20 years of service. He had his retirement ceremony at the Walter Reed Medical Center. At least that worked out for him. His years ahead were trying beyond comprehension.

Lundy spent his last two years on active duty undergoing a bone marrow transplant, attending medical appointments, being physically sick, and preparing for retirement. The transplant was not a pleasant time for Lundy; medical staff administered hallucinogenic drugs, the radiation made him ill, and he began to lose his thick, dark hair. Ellie spent as much time as possible visiting him in the hospital, attending Lundy's doctor's appointments, and applying cold compresses to his head. She had to adapt to preparing meals suited to his recovery. They were going through the motions of living but had become somewhat desensitized to the situation. Ellie continued to give as much as possible to her job, but realized she could not dedicate the time and energy required for continued success and ever-increasing responsibilities. She knew she had to plan her retirement at 20 years' service to the nation to care for Lundy until he took his last breath on this planet. She decided to retire and submitted the request for release from active duty in three years.

Ellie's mother passed away during this period, but she had given up on life after Ellie's sister died ten years prior. Carol was her mother's favorite; she always did the perfect, pleasing, and proper things. Her mother had already planned her funeral. The funeral ceremony went according to plan with all the right players involved. During the viewing, Ellie was surprised to see her mother without eyeglasses. She wore huge glasses with thick lenses the last time Ellie saw her. She was practically blind. Ellie's mother and sister entered her dreams periodically throughout her life. It was not until she was in her sixties that Ellie realized her mother and father were, in fact, good parents. They executed their responsibilities as parents following the conditioning their parents subjected them to. Ellie could now say, "I love you," forgiving herself for wrongful thoughts about her parents.

Chapter Seventeen - Westward to Texas

"There's no better place than Texas to start over."
—John Connelly

As retirement from the military approached for both, one crucial decision to make was deciding upon a location to live where Lundy could receive medical treatment at a military hospital, a hospital with the capability to provide the proper treatment for his terminal diagnosis. They considered three locations: remaining in the Washington D.C. area and continuing his treatment with the NIH, moving to Seattle for treatment at Madigan Army Hospital, or moving to Texas to receive treatment at Brooke Army Medical Center. Neither Ellie nor Lundy was particularly fond of the traffic or cost of living in the D.C. area, and they knew nothing about Seattle or the state of Washington. Lundy had served one tour early in his career in Texas, and Ellie was a native Texan, so the logical choice was to move to Texas.

Weather reports indicated record high temperatures

in Texas for the first day of March. They scheduled their move date for the third day of March; a two-foot snowfall overnight greeted them that morning in Washington, D.C. Because they did not know if the movers would arrive to pack and load the moving van, Ellie decided she needed to prepare in case they did. She retrieved the snow shovel from the trash where they had discarded it, thinking they would never need it in Texas, and shoveled a path through the snow from the front and back doors of the house to facilitate the movers when they loaded the moving van. Most of the physical work in the past couple of months was performed by Ellie since Lundy was too weak. She sensed his frustration in not being able to help. She was highly concerned about his ability to drive one of the cars in the two-car caravan from Virginia to Texas. He assured her he could do it. The movers arrived and had no difficulty navigating through the snow-filled cul-de-sac. After the movers pulled away with their belongings at the end of the day, Ellie and Lundy went to the hotel. They had secured the hotel room the previous day before leaving for Texas, contingent upon the roads being clear enough to travel.

The roads were clear the next day, and they pulled onto the road early, saying their farewells to Virginia forever. Lundy's brother was also in the military and assigned to a base in South Carolina. They had arranged to stop by for a brief visit since they had not seen each other in several years. There was good food and fun discussions about their visit to Germany. They were especially fond of one visit concerning Lundy's little niece, who kept yelling Lundy's name during the tour through the Neuschwanstein castle. It was good to see them, but after a couple of days in small living quarters with two small children running around, they were ready to hit the road. Although Ellie and Lundy loved children, they decided they did not want their own. She did not think she would make a good mother, an excuse for not wanting to raise children in potential poverty, a vivid childhood memory of her own. Even when her life became productive and successful, the fear remained. Now, she was too old for children. Lundy followed Ellie's lead and was comfortable with the childless nature of their marriage—a perfect union.

Lundy and Ellie headed south on Interstate 95 until they reached Interstate 10. Then they headed west to Texas. Lundy led the caravan with Ellie following. She kept up with him the entire distance, and they encountered no problems along the route, stopping when they needed a break or to sleep for the night. Despite driving-induced stress, Lundy felt well, a sign that his health was not an issue. They arrived at their new destination just before rush hour started. They stopped at a hotel where they had previously stayed to see if the city felt comfortable to them. Safely settled in, they reflected on how well everything fell into place during the long drive from Virginia. Tomorrow would be a day of rest, interspersed with planning their next steps and settling into their new environment.

First on the list was visiting the military hospital to complete the necessary paperwork for assigning Lundy an oncologist and scheduling a check-up for a health assessment, especially after the long trip. Ellie took advantage of the opportunity to register with a primary care doctor. Within a couple of weeks, Lundy had met with his new oncologist, who had coordinated with the National Institute of Health to obtain his medical records. Once a year, the Institute collected a blood sample and annotated the results in his case file. They still had an open case file for him. Ellie's visit with her doctor revealed she was still in good health. A visit to a newly assigned ophthalmologist revealed that the macular degeneration was not getting worse. A trip to the optometrist resulted in a new eyeglass prescription. She still needed assistance with reading at this point.

The second item on the list was meeting with the realtor they contacted before leaving Virginia, a referral from a friend. After a couple of weeks looking at houses, they decided to have a house built in a gated neighborhood north of town. It would have access to the major roads to get them to the hospital if necessary. They stayed in a furnished apartment a few minutes away while waiting for the completion of their house. Ellie and Lundy had never had a house built before and eagerly watched the building process. The builder completed their home in about five months. Now they had to wait three weeks for the movers to deliver their household goods from storage.

Moving with the military teaches service members how to organize, minimize, and keep only what they need. But unpacking is always fun, because you forget what you have. Movers came and went, and Ellie and Lundy were left to put things in order. They loved the house floor plan and its location. All of their belongings found a place in it. As they put away and organized things to suit them, they made mental notes of items they would like to add later. For now, Lundy and Ellie were content. The only remaining challenge was Lundy's health and the physical, mental, and emotional states he experienced. She, too, would face her own mental and emotional challenges in consonance with those he faced so bravely. It would not take her long to realize that he was much braver than she, more accepting of his fate, and more enlightened in his position as a spiritual leader.

Chapter Eighteen - **Rusty**

"If I could be half the person my dog is,
I'd be twice the human I am."
—Charles Yu.

A few months after settling into their new home, Lundy and Ellie began to feel a little bored; after all, they enjoyed having productive lives. In midlife, they thought they still had something to contribute to society. Lundy's doctors maintained his health with various medications; he was stable now and felt reasonably well. He even felt like he wanted to try to work part-time. He worked part-time for a few months, then he decided to take a chance on a full-time job offered to him. Ellie also found full-time employment. Within six months, they were both busy with their jobs, feeling productive again, delusional that life was finally stable. During an annual physical exam on her birthday, Ellie's doctor informed her that her bad cholesterol was too high, her thyroid was underactive, and her blood pressure was too high. For the first time in her life, she had to take maintenance medications for these issues. She often wondered if the stress she had experienced in the last couple of years was responsible for the decline in her health. The appointment with the ophthalmologist revealed her eyes were getting worse, but she did not pursue further treatment with a retina specialist.

In a couple of years, five years after the first autologous transplant, Lundy had a downturn with his health; the cancer was active again. He had a second transplant, this time with stem cells. This one was not as bad as the last; recovery was faster. Different medications were required to maintain a semblance of health, knowing that the slightest infection of any kind would be life-threatening, due to the decreased capability of his immune system. Lundy and Ellie had to be very careful in all aspects of life. The original prognosis of five remaining years of life had passed. Doctors were amazed that he was still alive and able to enjoy life with the help of medications and vigilance. Ellie continued to pretend that things would work out.

The first of many infection episodes struck Lundy about six months after the stem cell transplant. He and Ellie decided to spend a long weekend at the beach, one of their favorite pastimes. They had dinner out at a fine seafood restaurant the first night. At midnight, Lundy's vomiting and gagging in the bathroom awakened Ellie. After stabilizing his condition, she packed up and drove him back to the military hospital emergency room. After a week's stay in the hospital and numerous tests, the medical providers could not identify the cause of Lundy's infection. Was it merely due to a change in the environment? Was the seafood contaminated? No one knew. But both knew they were confronting an enemy they felt helpless against.

After the fifth trip to the emergency room, Ellie quit counting. On three occasions, he went directly to the ICU, one of which was on Thanksgiving Day. The doctors told her it was serious this time, and they did not know if Lundy would survive. She called her brother to be with her during this difficult time. However, Lundy's health improved, and in a week, they released him to go home.

Lundy's body had weakened considerably over the two years since the transplant. At Ellie's recommendation, he quit working altogether. Ellie continued to work to provide a diversion from taking care of him full-time. After a few weeks of staying home, Lundy decided he needed some company while Ellie was at work. He spent a couple of weeks researching which dog breed would be most compatible with him in his situation. Lundy decided he wanted a Cavalier King Charles Spaniel. They traveled to the breeder in Houston to retrieve their little bundle of joy. There were six pups in the litter; Lundy chose the one who did not follow the crowd, as he also doesn't follow the crowd. On the way home, they decided to name the puppy Rusty because of its red and white coloration; Lundy wanted to hold it all the way home, but Ellie suggested the puppy would probably be more comfortable on the car floor. She knew these two God's creations were going to be inseparable.

Rusty became the center of their attention, providing a much-needed diversion from their problems. He became a great companion for Lundy. He was always at Lundy's side and followed him everywhere. Rusty would develop separation anxiety episodes when Lundy left the house. Lundy and Ellie wanted to try another trip to the beach, and along came little Rusty. They took hundreds of photos of their center of attention; he had his own photo albums. The veterinarian suggested giving Rusty a Benadryl whenever they wanted to go out to dinner, and that seemed to work. But Lundy never wanted to leave him alone. Rusty liked riding in the car; he did not like the beach because he disliked getting wet.

Ellie was grateful for Rusty; he provided so much love to Lundy. One year was so bad, they called it "the year from hell." The doctors could not believe how he was still alive. During this year, Rusty was diagnosed with lymph cancer and given six to nine months to live, even after chemotherapy. Ellie could not begin to comprehend how Lundy would respond to the death of his beloved dog Rusty.

The day finally came when Lundy and Ellie knew it was time to put Rusty to sleep. Rusty had only slept in the last few days of his life; he did not eat. They were sitting on the couch when Rusty walked up to Lundy and looked up at him. Lundy picked him up, put him on the sofa, and stroked his fur. Ellie called the veterinarian and told him it was time. It was a solemn 15-minute trip to the veterinarian's office. They wanted to be with Rusty as the medication entered his little body, and he went limp. Lundy's knees had already weakened; Ellie grabbed his shoulders, and they went home. They had made arrangements for Rusty's cremation, and someone would contact them when the ashes were ready to be retrieved. Neither of them shed any tears in front of the other. They did not sleep that night. The next morning, Lundy said, "I cannot go through that again." Trying to be strong and stoic for Lundy, Ellie kept her emotional turmoil in check. Two weeks after Rusty left their lives, she went to the patio one evening, sat in a chair, and cried for an hour. She knew Lundy cried during the day while she was at work. He told her that she and Rusty had become close during the last year because he had been sick and had many hospital stays. Ellie agreed.

A few weeks after Rusty's euthanasia, they received his cremains, put them in the closet, and Lundy never looked at them or spoke of Rusty again. In a week or so, Lundy said he wanted to get another dog, another Cavalier King Charles Spaniel with the same coloration as Rusty. Ellie grew concerned about Lundy's emotional state. She explained to him that they could get a dog that looked much like Rusty, but it would have a completely different personality. They discussed this with their veterinarian, who reinforced what Ellie had stated. They called the same breeder and got another dog. They got a female dog this time. She was a breeder, but since her litters were small, the breeder agreed to sell her to Lundy and Ellie. Lundy named her Sara, and they became fast friends. Ellie could tell no difference in Lundy's attachment to Sara compared to Rusty; however, Ellie did not develop the same bond she had with Rusty. One of Lundy's final remarks to Ellie before his soul left his body was, "Take care of Sara."

Chapter Nineteen - The Last Days

"Memories are the treasures that we keep locked deep within the storehouse of our souls."
—Becky Aligada

Over the first five to six years of Lundy's diagnosis, their friends ceased to call, send cards, or communicate in any way. Lundy and Ellie, receiving minimal physical support from their families due to distance, relied on phone calls for strength and encouragement; they became a closer team, separating themselves from the rest of the world, except for medical personnel involved with his care and people with whom they worked. He often remarked to Ellie that he was sorry he had created an isolated environment for her; she did not concern herself with his thoughts but tried to reassure him that she was at peace with their life, under the circumstances, and felt no concern about the lack of socialization with other people. Characteristically outgoing, she became more absorbed with her life and its challenges. Nonetheless, they spent the remaining seven years of his life as productively and engaged as possible.

One day, Lundy greeted Ellie at the door when she returned home after work. "Did you see it?" He asked. "See what?" Was her response. He led her into the garage and showed her the crumpled hood on his car. He explained that he ran into the back of the vehicle in front of him at the car wash; he hit the wrong pedal when moving forward in line. That cost them the repair of the other vehicle, as well as the repair of their own. She decided it was time for the "give me the keys" conversation. She knew this would be another blow to his independence. Stressing that he was becoming a danger to others on the road and himself, Ellie presented her position with patience and understanding. Little did she know that she would face the same decision one day. Lundy agreed—no more driving for him. They traded in their two cars and bought a new SUV that allowed Lundy to get in and out of it more easily.

Ellie went through the motions of commuting to work, fulfilling her responsibilities, and supporting Lundy's physical, emotional, and mental needs. She used the vacation days she accrued at work to take Lundy to medical appointments, sit with him in the ICU, or attend rehabilitation events. Vacations, short road trips, and outdoor activities dwindled to non-existent. Lundy walked with Ellie each day after work for exercise. They walked a one-mile route through the neighborhood; Lundy initially used a cane and later transitioned to a walker as time progressed. Recreation consisted mainly of going out to dinner occasionally; movies were a special treat. The one last trip to the beach never came to fruition.

Still, after all their years together, Lundy and Ellie loved, respected, and honored each other. Lundy was the perfect patient. The only complaint he ever made was when he was required to undergo a test requiring an IV. She was standing beside his bed when he spoke in a hushed, tired voice, "I am so tired of all this." All she could do was respond, "I know." Ellie exhibited moments of frustration and unkindness; immediately realizing it, she apologized, trying not to be too hard on herself. The years were good because they still had each other; that was all that mattered.

Chapter Twenty
- Gone, But Never Forgotten

"Life is eternal, and love is immortal, and death is only a Horizon; and a horizon is nothing save the limit of our sight."
—Rossiter Worthington Raymond

Ellie accompanied Lundy to what turned out to be the last office visit with the oncologist. The doctor broached the subject of hospice care to assist Ellie because Lundy required close observation by a trained medical professional. Lundy, now realizing the severity of the situation, agreed to hospice care, remarking, "This is such a final move." Ellie made arrangements for Lundy's care during the day. Ellie took care of him in the evening. Then he contracted another intestinal infection requiring hospitalization. By this time, Ellie realized she was no longer physically, emotionally, or mentally capable of caring for Lundy. She was not sleeping; she was anxious, on the verge of a breakdown, and needed to focus on her health. After bringing him home from the hospital, she shared her thoughts regarding her participation in his care. She asked him if he would be receptive to moving to an assisted living facility.

Calmly and tenderly, Lundy responded favorably to her request. She had him transferred to a facility equipped to meet his medical needs. He selected the facility, and Ellie moved his meager belongings to his room in the assisted living facility. The night before the move, she asked him what he would like for his last dinner at home. She already knew, before asking, that he would want spaghetti with meat sauce, as it was his favorite dish; the sauce was one of Ellie's creations. The room was small with a single medical bed, a television stand, and a small chest of drawers for his clothing. A doctor visited him each day. The nursing staff was competent and kind. Ellie visited him every day during lunch and after work. They missed each other terribly; an emptiness entered Ellie's soul. She could not imagine how Lundy felt because he never talked about his plight; he just endured.

After three weeks in the facility, Lundy developed another infection, so the medical staff evacuated him to a military hospital. The attending physician determined it was an intestinal infection, but could not determine the specific cause unless Lundy underwent a scope. The physician discouraged this option because the procedure would probably kill Lundy. Everyone concerned made the necessary arrangements to send Lundy to a hospice hospital for the remainder of his life. On the way to the hospice facility in an ambulance, Ellie gently stroked Lundy's head as the ambulance's emergency medical personnel monitored his vital signs and managed the oxygen flow. She was a zombie at this point, silently pleading for someone, anyone, to provide her a lifeline.

The nursing staff in the hospice hospital had specialized experience with enabling patients nearing the end of their earthly journey to do so comfortably, as well as comforting the family as they cope with an expected permanent loss of a loved one. She could not describe the kindness and gentleness exhibited by the hospice care staff; people who enter the hospice medical care profession receive a divine calling and support. Ellie explained to the physician that she did not want Lundy to be in pain; he assured her that Lundy would not experience any pain. Lundy's comforting words would remain with her the rest of her life: "Thank you for letting me share this journey with you." Ellie felt complete peace in that slim moment, if only for the blink of an eye.

Ellie contacted her brother to inform him that Lundy would be passing. Lee and Sue came as soon as they could and remained with Ellie in her home until the end. They visited Lundy every day, although he could not communicate with them. The nurse told them that Lundy could probably hear what they were saying but could not respond. Ellie and Sue left Lundy's side one afternoon to arrange the cremation and burial at the national military cemetery. Four days after entering the hospital, Lundy passed away at 12:30 A.M. on a Friday. Ellie and her small family had just gotten to bed the night before when she received a call at 1:00 A.M. informing her that Lundy had passed. All three of them dressed and went back to the hospital to be in attendance when the funeral home personnel came to remove the body.

Her brother and sister-in-law remained with Ellie for a few days afterward. Concerned about Ellie's emotional state, they drove her to the doctor for anxiety and depression medications. They helped her pack Lundy's clothing and medical devices to donate to the Disabled Veterans Association. The state statutory wait period for cremation ended, and the funeral home that removed Lundy's body from the hospice hospital cremated his body. There was no memorial service or military graveside ceremony, per Lundy's request. Ellie became lucid enough for her family to return home.

Ellie and her friend–and lifeline at this point–Elaine, watched while military personnel placed Lundy's cremains in the columbarium at the national cemetery. She said goodbye to Lundy, and then the door to the columbarium vault was closed.

PART III: Life Goes On

Chapter Twenty-One - Emerging From the Depths of Despair

"No matter how hard the past, you can always begin again."
—Buddha

Ellie eventually grew mentally numb reading all the condolence cards and notes that were variations of the same message with different words. She grew weary of well-meaning condolences, which she perceived as empty words of encouragement. "You will find a new normal," or "Lundy is in a better place now," were her least favorite. No one could understand what was happening in her mind as she sorted through a mental dialogue, weighing how she would continue living without him. She felt that until one goes through grieving for a person that was so dearly loved and appreciated, no one should have the right to advise someone grieving on how to manage it. She thought it was callous and shallow. No one ever offered to sit in pure, peaceful silence with her or hold her hand. Her body was functioning, but her mind was void of external and internal stimuli. At the beginning of each day, she would have to think about what day it was, what tasks she needed to perform to settle Lundy's affairs, and when she could face the task of returning to work.

She took a two-week absence from work, mainly because she did not want to face people who still had lives with loved ones. She finalized Lundy's will with the probate court, provided death certificates to all who required one, paid the final assisted living statement, took care of Sara as Lundy instructed, and reorganized the closet and drawers to accommodate her things—she now had so much more space. But the emptiness would not go away. Frequently, she would pound her head on the kitchen cabinet and wail, hoping to oust the indescribable pain permeating her soul.

Returning to work provided some relief. Ellie could focus, if only in short spurts, on something other than responding to waves of grief that swept over her occasionally. Sometimes, one co-worker would come into her office to see how she was doing. Once, she admitted that she felt her purpose for living was gone; she had spent so many years prioritizing Lundy's care over her own that she had left nothing for herself. Weekends and holidays presented increased difficulty in responding to her feelings of loneliness and a sense of purpose.

Grief counsellors recommend that a person who has lost a spouse wait at least a year before selling their house. Ellie was ready to sell in six months. Living in the house was much too painful, and she did not feel safe, even with a security system in a gated community. The real estate agent helped her secure a fabulous apartment in a reputable part of town with a secure, established neighborhood. The house sold within twenty-four hours to the real estate agent's uncle. She felt relieved that it would be going to a trusted person. Now, Ellie faced the task of downsizing to move into an apartment about half the size of the house. Ellie did not realize it, but something was moving her forward; an unseen power guided and directed her thoughts and actions.

Downsizing proved to be a time-consuming endeavor. But parting with stuff was not as painful as Ellie thought, possibly because she was ready to stop expending so much energy on the effort. Rather than having an estate sale as most people do when they downsize, hoping to recoup some monetary compensation for this abrupt change in their lives, she donated to various organizations, including Disabled Veterans, Goodwill Industries, and other charitable organizations. She did not consider the tax-exempt status of the donations. As each piece of furniture and other household items left the house, Ellie embraced the good times associated with them and let them go, never to be thought of again. However, one major decision required some reflection. What should she do with Rusty's cremains? This was the last item with which she departed. Lundy never mentioned what they should do with them. She decided to scatter his ashes over the back yard where he enjoyed running around, barking at the birds and butterflies. Lundy would have agreed with this decision. The remaining furniture and household items provided the comfort she required in her new abode.

Chapter Twenty-Two - **Sight Loss Event 3**

"Often when you think you're at the end of something, you're at the beginning of something else."
—Fred Rogers

While living in the apartment, she had a follow-up appointment with her retina specialist, since she had just recently had a birthday. The macular degeneration in her right eye had developed into the "wet" kind, which meant the tiny capillaries surrounding the retinal drusen had begun leaking blood. This development was a serious event requiring her to receive bi-monthly injections, containing a cutting-edge medication, in the right eye. The drusen in the left retina were still "dry." This event was the first time that she was concerned about her vision, to the point that the doctor provided her with literature and a CD containing information on the condition, as well as a projected development diagnosis over several years, concluding with the fact that there is no cure for the disease. The injections continued for about three years until the retina specialist decided to stop them for a while, as he believed the blood seepage had stopped. Her visual acuity in her right eye had significantly decreased. Now, she would have to wait to see if the condition returned.

As the disease progresses, central vision deteriorates. At the end stage, there is no central vision. Years later, Ellie told a friend, "I will not be able to see your face." She would see a gray patch, which could be of any shape; however, it did not affect her peripheral vision. Ellie would spend many years of appointments with her retina specialist receiving injections at variable intervals.

At this point, Ellie realized she would lose her eyesight, and life would change drastically. Losing her eyesight would be a life-altering event. The fear of responding to this inevitable event eroded Ellie's confidence in moving forward with her life. After three years of living alone in an apartment without close friends or neighbors, she searched for a retirement community that offered independent living and assisted living. She felt that she would need that environment when her central vision left, the timing of which no one could predict.

After spending many hours researching online for independent living and assisted living facilities in the city where she currently lived, Ellie found that the quantity and quality of retirement communities were sufficient, providing an excellent opportunity to choose one from many options. She toured and interviewed the marketing departments of five communities. She made two visits to each one. The first round of visits produced a long list of questions to ask during the second interview. She learned much about continuing care communities and which ones did not offer continuing care. This process made her realize she was an aging citizen and could see her remaining years as few—another foreign revelation. Ellie moved into a retirement community with retired military officers and their spouses. In her self-induced, fear-filled mind, she thought she would feel more comfortable and more at home with people of similar experiences and values. She signed the contract with a move-in date of October 30.

While Elle reflected and planned for another relocation, she decided to retire early. At this point, she was miserable in her job, feeling like her life had hit a brick wall, and she could not move forward. One day at work, after a frustrating discussion with her boss, she sat down at her desk and, almost on the edge of tears, a voice in her mind said plainly and calmly, "retire." Of course! She could retire early, turning another page in her life. She gave a 90-day notice, which coincided with the day she would move into her new apartment in a reputed retirement community. She had three months to finalize and execute plans for a significant change in her life.

Although the military organization where she worked wanted to acknowledge her retirement departure at a special social event, she informed them that she did not want fanfare. She devoted 33 years of her life to the military, 20 years on active duty, and 13 years as a military civilian employee. Approximately two weeks after she retired, she received an award through the mail. Without anger, she asked a friend still working in the organization to return the award to the sender without any response. It just did not matter. She knew that she had performed well, enabling the organization to ensure the fielding of critical technology and prompting a similar shift in thinking about all the military awards she had received through the years.

Chapter Twenty-Three - **The Tourist**

"It is good to have an end to journey toward; but it is the journey that matters in the end."
—Ernest Hemingway

Ellie's move to the retirement community was easier since she had already downsized before moving into her current apartment. The new apartment was the same size as the current one. She would be comfortable among the material things that added to that feeling. As the youngest resident to move into the retirement community, she was a novelty, so Ellie had to contend with unwanted attention. The self-appointed and elected resident leaders solicited her to join various committees and contribute to the community through numerous volunteer activities. Feeling obligated, she took her time to decide how she would contribute to the community. Serving others had always been her focus in response to societal expectations. She volunteered her time to help residents in nursing care and assisted living. She pushed wheelchairs around the corridors to show disabled residents the beautiful Christmas decorations, occasionally drove people to doctors' appointments, and served on a few committees, with landscape maintenance being her favorite. Her main effort was serving as the community newsletter editor for five years.

As editor, Ellie had the opportunity to write articles, conduct interviews, and offer opinions. She would orchestrate the collection of noteworthy contributions from the residents. Writing had always been a joy for her. Although she studied science in college, she always wondered how different her life would have been if she had followed the advice of one high school English teacher who encouraged her to study journalism. Nonetheless, she was happy with the way her life turned out. Not many people had the opportunities she grabbed with gusto to explore life to its fullest. Ellie successfully digitized the newspaper, enabling residents to view it on the community website, bringing it into the 21st century. At the end of five years, she resigned as editor without remorse. She retired from volunteering altogether. Not feeling guilty for her selfish decision, she desired to travel while still in good health and could see the world with her eyes. She did not want to adhere to a constant deadline.

Ellie joined an organization that provided educational and travel opportunities for senior citizens in her city. The organization arranged group travel, so she did not have to plan the trip and would have other people she knew with whom to travel. She attended many classes on various subjects, but grew tired of the monotony of the subjects after a couple of years. Lundy had been her travel buddy; now, she did not have one. During their travels, she and Lundy would frequently encounter travel groups and remark on how lucky they were to have the opportunity to choose what they wanted to do, rather than rely on a tour guide. After her first trip, which she had arranged through a reputable travel company, she came to appreciate the importance of a tour guide. Granted, tour guides would take the group to typical tourist spots, but they would frequently provide historical or interesting stories about the sites they visited.

The first trip with this group was to Switzerland. Ellie had lived in Germany for six years and had visited many countries, but had only visited Switzerland once. It was just an overnight stay on the way to Austria. She and Lundy had pulled into Lucerne late in the day, found a luxury hotel for the night, and had a wonderful dinner in a famous restaurant nearby. They slept on a round bed with a mirror above it, and she had to ask Lundy what the bidet was. The travel group stayed in a mountain hotel in a village below the Eiger. It was incredibly picturesque. Cows grazed on the hillsides, bells clanging with each bite of grass. The hotel was old, but very comfortable, and the meals were excellent. With many excursions on the agenda, the most memorable was the trip to the top of the Eiger. The temperature at the summit was freezing, but the small group had dressed for cold temperatures. Many from the group had opted out of the excursion because it would be too cold, and they did not feel comfortable going to a high altitude—wimps, Ellie thought. There was a visitor center at the top with films of various kinds. For example, one film was about how a tunnel was cut into the mountain for a train to reach the top. Ellie ventured out alone to a location with a platform where you could see the path of debris left by a moving glacier. She felt so alive in the cold at 13,000 feet. Maybe it was due to oxygen deprivation, but she felt relatively peaceful, as if God was holding her in His hand. This experience moved her so much that she wrote an article about it in the community newsletter. Ellie and her travel buddy made friends with another twosome, with whom they hung out. They called themselves the Swiss Chicks. They enjoyed lunch each month and exchanged Christmas gifts for almost 15 years. Sadly, the relationship changed when one of them began to experience health issues and had to move to an assisted living facility. Life keeps you on your toes and teaches you how to respond to various changes.

Other trips with this organization included excursions to Palo Duro Canyon in the Texas Panhandle, the Fort Worth Stockyards, Montreal, Quebec, and Niagara Falls in Canada, as well as other notable sights. They also took miscellaneous day trips to tour lesser-traveled sites free from tourists. While all these trips were educational and fun, Ellie grew weary of traveling with the same group on each trip. They were all members of the organization and traveled together; they also saw each other in different classes offered during the week. She wanted to expand her interaction with various people, hoping to find a variety of mental stimulation. She decided to try a different travel agency for seniors, one with female solo travelers.

Ellie found a travel agency that advertised a two-week trip to Cuba. The President of the United States had recently authorized U.S. citizens in organized groups to travel to Cuba. With national politics, Ellie theorized that the window of opportunity could close after the next general election. She cast her fear of traveling to a developing, communist country aside and signed up for the trip during the Christmas and New Year holiday period. In a few months, she departed Miami on an American Airlines plane and landed an hour later in Holguin, Cuba. The travel group was more diverse, comprising approximately 50 travelers from many different states in the U.S. and one from Canada. Ellie knew no one, but looked forward to talking to a distinct group, hoping to find interesting people with varied backgrounds.

Ellie decided not to have a roommate on the trip, unsure of how receptive that person would be to a creature of habit with many idiosyncrasies. They spent the first week riding a bus across the northern part of Cuba into the central part of the country. Lodging along the route was interesting and comfortable, but did not meet the same standards as those in the United States. The hotels were mainly government-owned, small hotels in the center of a city. Dining offered opportunities for a unique cuisine, featuring a lot of seafood prepared simply with a blend of spices unfamiliar to the American palate. Because the Cuban government was beginning to adopt some Western ways (capitalism), 10 percent of the population now had their own businesses; otherwise, Cuban businesses were government-managed and operated. The group ate at privately owned restaurants, and the owners were very enthusiastic about the American patronage, catering to their every wish.

The bus was modern with a nice intercom system that the guide used prolifically. The guide spoke English very well and did a superb job of educating the group on all the stops along the way that the Cuban government wanted them to see. One indoctrination was a village medical center tour showcasing socialist medicine. The doctor and nurse in attendance explained that the village residents received excellent health care from their clinic. Most larger villages in Cuba have this medical system. The government is proud of its medical system and the health care professionals responsible for its operation. The doctor explained that Cuba had offered to send doctors to the U.S. to help with medical needs related to hurricane emergencies in states affected along the Gulf of Mexico. The U.S. declined the offers. On the last day of the ground trip, the tour guide explained that the Cuban government was a socialist democracy rather than a communist one. He thanked the group for visiting Cuba. The bus dropped the group off at the port in Santiago de Cuba to embark on a cruise along the southern coast to Havana.

The vessel was old and drab, and the group questioned its seaworthiness. The guide told a few travelers that the boat had sunk at one time. They prayed it would get them and the other three hundred passengers to their destination. Each evening, a group dinner was held in the dining room; the food was average. They all lost weight during the entire trip because of the food. A few port stops en route provided a further influx of American dollars into the economy. One stop included a tour of an old sugar cane plantation; the Cuban government had not maintained the property well. But then, of course, had they done that, it would have been a tribute to capitalism. Finally, the boat, still intact, reached Havana, which was once known as the Paris of the Caribbean at the height of its wealth from the enormous sugar cane industry. The hotel where they stayed was very nice; the group took walking excursions through the city for two days. Havana was a charming place—modern and busy.

The group's last lunch was at a privately owned restaurant about twenty minutes from the hotel. No one remembered the meal since it was like all their other meals. When the group was preparing to leave, the guide informed them that the bus had a maintenance issue. The guide arranged alternative transportation to get them back to town. They saw several brightly painted, vintage automobiles when they walked through the restaurant door to leave. Each person selected the car they wanted to ride in and ran toward it. Ellie chose a bright pink 1956 Chevy convertible. All the cars were convertibles. She and three other old ladies had a wonderful time riding to the hotel.

The Havana airport was small compared to American standards. But it was swamped with people trying to get on the next plane. There was a central area where everyone congregated to await their plane. The group's American Airlines plane was 45 minutes late. The airport did not have organized queues for exiting onto the tarmac where the plane would land. The airport personnel changed the gates a total of four times. The place was in chaos. After waiting for a couple of hours in an unorganized line that included travel group members and others, as well as guides bribing airport officials, and waiting for an American Airlines plane that was late, the group finally boarded the plane. They heard a huge collective sigh of relief as soon as the airplane lifted off, heading for Miami. Even though Ellie was glad she went on the trip, she had no desire to return. The experience taught her that people are the same whether she had known them for a while or had just met them during a short trip. All human beings share the same characteristics.

Chapter Twenty-Four - One Dog, Three Cats, and Seven Chickens

"The magic thing about home is that it feels good to leave, and it feels even better to come back."
—Wendy Wunder

Instead of traveling by airplane, bus, or train, Ellie decided to do some road trips. Simultaneously, she embarked on a new experience—house-sitting. After registering as a house sitter with a nationwide house-sitting service, she selected two locations to sit homes for people on vacation. It was a new way to see more of the country, meet new people, and provide a service. After phone conversations with the selected homeowners, both parties felt comfortable with their decisions. Ellie did not know these people. The house-sitting service did not require background checks. She had no idea what sort of neighborhood the homeowners lived in.

On the other hand, it must have been unsettling for the people handing over the care of their home to a stranger. These people did not know Ellie; however, she provided them with a photocopy of her driver's license and retired military ID. The latter cinched the deal. Ellie and the homeowners had to establish mutual trust.

Southern California was the location of Ellie's first house-sitting service. She was responsible for caring for the house a retired parole officer owned and caring for her little dog for 10 days. Ellie knew what to expect for three or four days when traveling through West Texas, New Mexico, Arizona, and southern California for the fourth time. She was still comfortable traveling solo. This trip also brought back fond memories of Lundy and friends, Adam and Barbara, who lived in Tucson. The two of them had invited her to stay a couple of days on the way to California. About an hour outside Tucson, as she admired the scenery and looked at the clear, blue sky, Ellie noticed that the vision in her right eye became distorted for a second or two. She thought nothing of it as it cleared up and did not return immediately.

Visiting her friends helped break the monotony of being on the road, and she enjoyed spending time with them. Lundy and Ellie became friends with Adam and Barbara during their second tour in California. Initially, Adam was Ellie's boss, and their friendship developed a few years later. When she informed him that she and Lundy would be getting married in Lake Tahoe the following weekend, Adam told her that he would like to see them get married in the chapel down the street from where they worked. She agreed and informed Lundy of the change in plans. On the wedding day, while Ellie and Lundy were receiving marriage counseling from the minister, all the military members assigned to their units, wearing their dress blue uniforms, silently entered the chapel. When Ellie and Lundy started to walk down the chapel aisle to greet the best man, matron of honor, and the minister, the only people they expected to see, they were greeted by a chapel full of people. Ellie felt Lundy immediately tense up, but they both made it through the surprise ceremony without screwing it up. Afterwards, Adam and Barbara treated them to a wedding reception at their house. This memorable experience was a topic of discussion on many occasions.

Enjoying a high moment after the visit with Adam and Barbara, Ellie headed toward the destination house near San Bernardino. The homeowner, a middle-aged woman leaving on a cruise the following morning with her boyfriend, lived alone with her little Scottish Terrier, Max. It was a smaller, older home located in a well-established neighborhood. Taking care of the house and Max would be a welcome change of pace for her, but that was what she yearned for. The owner left the next morning before dawn. Max found his way to Ellie's bed, and she told him to lie down on the rug beside the bed. He obeyed, and that was his sleeping place for ten days. Ellie enjoyed walking Max twice each day. She enjoyed walking in the quiet neighborhood, in the clean air, and getting some exercise. Max loved his walks, and his internal clock would let Ellie know when it was time to go. The home had a fence around it, allowing him to wander outside. Ellie bought a few groceries at a nearby neighborhood grocery store. She ate easy, simple meals. When the time came to prepare the house for the owner's arrival, Ellie cleaned the house and bought flowers to greet the owner upon her return. Ellie was pleased that this first experience was pleasant for everyone.

Ellie had another house-sitting gig in a week, just north of Tucson, located in the foothills of the mountains just west of the city. She decided to follow the old Route 66 on her way back to Arizona to kill some time sightseeing. She left the first house in the rearview mirror and headed north to San Bernardino to hit Route 66 east. Route 66 had multiple routes east, depending on the construction year and the terrain considered for the routes. This route would take Ellie from San Bernardino to Barstow, Needles, and finally Arizona, paralleling Interstate 40. She made it to Barstow on the first day, just before a Santa Anna windstorm. She hoped she would make it there safely, as the dust rapidly made driving more difficult. She finally checked into an old 1950s motel. By the time she unloaded her luggage, the dust was so thick that she could not see the street; it was getting darker as the sun set, and dust covered the little remaining light. She managed to order a pizza delivery, since she couldn't go out into the storm to walk or drive to town when she could not see through the dust. After watching television for a while, she went to bed, hoping to make up for the time tomorrow that she had lost.

The next morning, dust from the windstorm covered Ellie's car, and sand piles surrounded the vehicle's tires in the parking lot. The storm still delivered dust particles on the wind, permeating the air and obscuring all objects in its path. There would be no traveling today; weather reports indicated the storm would break by the next morning. Ellie was dust-bound. The windstorm set her back on her journey and would affect her sightseeing plans. The wind abated during the night, leaving piles of accrued dust on the cars and buildings. She walked down the street to a small coffee shop where she ordered a cup of coffee and a pastry, which she leisurely consumed. She then cleaned off as much dust as she could from outside the car, hoping the dust had not affected the engine compartment. By mid-morning, she was on the road. The road across the desert to Barstow was the original Route 66, evidently well-traveled in its earlier existence. The next day, Ellie visited the Route 66 Museum and the railroad museum. She was surprised by the massive rail yard complex, which displayed more than a dozen rail tracks used to transport railcars loaded with goods from California, headed east and vice versa. Both museums were interesting, but any information provided was always appreciated.

The drive through the Mojave Desert to Needles awakened her imagination to the time when this country was part of the old Santa Fe Trail. The driving distance from Barstow was short, giving Ellie time to see parts of Needles. She stayed overnight in an old Route 66 hotel with no elevators and gaudy furnishings. The final stretch the next day brought her to Flagstaff, where she hoped to sightsee for a few days. The scenery changed from shades of gray to green as the elevation increased when approaching the alpine city. Ellie had two free days before reporting to her second house-sitting job in Tucson. She spent the first day exploring the old city. She devoted the second day to seeing the Meteor Crater and Petrified Forest National Park east of Flagstaff. By this time, Ellie was ready to reach her scheduled destination and stay put for a while.

She arrived at her next house sitting stop right on

time, after meandering through the hills with dead-end roads, sparse housing, and poor signage. The homeowners, a middle-aged couple who had retired early and lived off the grid, had escaped to Arizona for a slower, quieter pace. The modern double-car garage stucco house, built atop a hill, had a fantastic view where one could see for miles in all directions. As Ellie entered the house, she was pleased at the modern conveniences, but the old tube TV was out of place in the decor. The couple explained that they rarely watched TV and hoped the lack of this entertainment would not burden her. Scurrying up to meet her was their little Chihuahua/Terrier mix. Acknowledging the animal with a pat on the head and a stroke on the back, she was familiar with this breed and knew she would have to muster patience and vigilance while caring for him. One cat sauntered lazily to the group investigating the noise that had interrupted its nap; within a few seconds, it nestled into its favorite chair to continue its vigilance. Soon, two more cats entered the fray, brushing against Ellie's leg to receive accustomed attention. She asked if any more animals required her attention. Then, the couple took Ellie through the beautifully tiled patio to a fenced area with an aluminum shed covering. Netting extended from the fence to the lip of the covering. They opened a latched entrance to the area, instructed Ellie to follow them, and introduced her to the seven named chickens. She was not opposed to caring for chickens, as collecting eggs was one of her childhood chores when she lived on the farm. She breathed a sigh of relief that there was no rooster. She was terrified of roosters. So, here Ellie was, housesitting on a mountain in the middle of nowhere, and charged with the health, care, and well-being of one dog, three cats, and seven chickens.

After meeting the family, the humans returned to the house, where Ellie received a reference book containing details on what she needed to do. To ensure she understood her duties, the couple reviewed the instructions with her—they were very conscientious in tending to their responsibilities. They even relayed information on the personalities of each animal. She already had the dog pegged. Feeding the cats would present no problem; they are not messy and tend to care for themselves. Even though not a cat lover, Ellie could handle this for a few days. The chickens were a different matter. They were noisy, messy, and required extra security since they were the favorite prey for mountain carnivores. She did chores in the mornings. Ellie enjoyed walking the dog up and down the hills and seeing the terrain up close and personally. Next, she would feed the animals. She collected the eggs at 10:00 AM, placed them in egg containers, and put them in the refrigerator. The couple told her that if she wanted eggs, she could help herself with them, so she enjoyed an egg each day for breakfast. She watered the plants on the patio, front porch, and in the flower beds around the house every three days. She spent afternoons running errands in town, sightseeing in local areas, reading, playing with the dog, and enjoying the peace and quiet that the environment afforded.

Ellie tried sleeping without the air conditioning one night because the nighttime temperatures were cool. Just as she was beginning to drift off, she heard a noise outside the bedroom window. Bolting out of bed, she sneaked into the front part of the house to ensure she had locked the front and back doors, and they were. She stood still for a few minutes, listening for any strange noise. Suddenly, the chickens began clucking. They continued for a couple of minutes before going silent. Ellie thought the object making the noise might have been a bobcat. The homeowners had told her that bobcats were a common pest in the area, and they had previously killed some chickens. Another possibility was that a noncitizen had crossed the border, a short distance from her location. After half an hour, she decided to turn the air conditioning back on, close the window, and try to get some sleep.

When the couple returned ten days later, Ellie did not leave the bed at 2:00 AM to greet them. She had already packed all her things. She left early the next morning at 7:00 AM to travel to her friends' home again to stay with Barbara, while Adam took a short trip to Denver to visit his sister. She left the owners a bouquet and a thank-you card. Considering everything that could have happened, the only adverse event was that the dog managed to get into her luggage and eat the granola bars she kept on hand.

After the short three-day visit with Barbara, Ellie drove north from Tucson through the beautiful canyons of the Pueblo. Picking up Route 66 again, Ellie headed East on Interstate 40. She headed to Oklahoma City, where she drove south to Arkansas to visit her brother before heading home to Texas. After six weeks of driving, house-sitting, and playing tourist, she was ready to go home.

Immediately upon her return, she went to her military retina specialist to relay to him the experience she had with her vision on the way to California, only to be informed that he had left the Army to go into private practice. The army had no replacement for him in the foreseeable future. As he was the only retina specialist on the staff of the flagship military hospital, Ellie was on the verge of panic, so she explained her plight and inquired what to do next. The medical personnel gave her a list of local retina specialists to find a replacement. Of course, she knew none of the doctors, but after doing some online research, she picked a name, made an appointment, and visited her new doctor three weeks later. The doctor-patient chemistry was evident; that relationship would remain marked by vision challenges for the rest of her life. After a battery of scans, he informed Ellie that the right eye exhibited blood leakage and that she must resume the medication injections immediately. She had been through the injection drill before and knew what to expect, but she did not expect his encouraging words just before he injected the needle: "You are so brave."

Chapter Twenty-Five - Around the World in 21 Days

"I am not the same, having seen the moon shine on the other side of the world."
—Mary Anne Radmacher

Ellie wanted to give herself a special birthday present when she turned 70 in a couple of years. She decided to go for broke and signed up for a trip around the world by private jet with a reputable travel agency. She and Lundy had planned to take such a trip after they retired; she knew he would be with her as she journeyed across the planet. It took several months to obtain all the security documentation, medical requirements, clothing, and other items required for the excursion. She knew the number of luggage pieces she could take would be limited, so careful planning went into packing her wardrobe. The travel agency provided a backpack and carry-on luggage; the backpack was especially useful. It became a separate appendage to her torso. Online research revealed that the weather where she would be traveling in October was near perfect. Due to her organizational ability, her packing effort was nearly flawless, and she was ready with all the weather contingencies planned.

Her only concern was her vision; what if it got worse in a country with virtually no medical care, especially eye care? This fear manifested itself on many occasions as Ellie debated whether to travel or engage in an event that would not be near a retinal specialist. Her vision was beginning to control her life. But with all things in perfect alignment so far, Ellie felt peaceful. This trip would be a once-in-a-lifetime event. It was now or never.

Seventy-five people from various locations in the United States, and one man from Australia, headed to the trip's starting point, Washington, D.C. They spent one night in D.C. at the Hay-Adams Hotel. Ellie was impressed with how well-organized the travel agency was. When they entered the hotel, a trip guide met everyone in the group and showed them to their rooms. After a wonderful dinner at a restaurant down the street, tourists and their guides met in a conference room to review the trip details, focusing on the next day's activities. Similar events occurred each evening to keep guests informed. After a quick breakfast the next morning, the guide directed everyone into buses to take them to a special area at Regan International Airport. The guide escorted them through security as a group; airport personnel separated their baggage from them and loaded it onto the plane. This security process and the baggage handling procedure occurred in every airport they went through. The travel agency handled all the guests' affairs. Ellie had never experienced such special attention while traveling. It was great. After completing the security process, they exited a special terminal just for this flight. The buses took them to the tarmac to board the plane. The plane was a 747 jet, chartered with a British company. They had to walk up the steps to the plane's entrance. When Ellie entered the plane, she was overwhelmed by the luxurious interior. The airplane contained reconfigured, outsized leather seats; two on each side of the aisle. She thought this was better than the first-class seating of any plane she had flown on. Within 15-20 minutes, the 75 guests, tour guides, other travel agency personnel, and the plane crew settled in. It was time to take off.

The first stop was Peru. Ellie used the flight time to become acquainted with her seatmate, who served in that capacity for the first half of the expedition. The two of them occupied the same seat during that time. During the second half of the expedition, each solo guest sat in a different seat with a different guest as their mate. This arrangement allowed solo travelers to develop a relationship with their seatmate, who could become their trip buddy. While they traveled to Peru, an international chef served the guests lunch prepared in the small kitchen. Two of the flight crew were designated food servers. They provided menus to each guest, allowing them to make their selections, and gave their orders to the chef. The chef prepared the food with fresh ingredients native to Peru; the same process occurred at the other locations where they landed. Each menu had two main course selections from which to choose. All food consumed on the plane was superb, especially the desserts. Dining on the airplane allowed Ellie to open her mind to the possibilities of enjoying foods from other countries. Ellie kept thinking how much Lundy would have loved to travel on this trip; he was also a foodie, ready to travel with little notice.

The plane landed in Lima at dusk. Rapidly, they split into two groups. One group selected Machu Picchu from the itinerary, and the other group traveled to the Inca ruins along the northern coast of Lima. The Machu Picchu group boarded a smaller plane, which took them to Cusco. The day soon turned into night, so Ellie didn't get to see much, but she was beginning to tire a little by now and looked forward to going to the hotel room. There was a thirty-minute bus ride from the airport to the hotel. Ellie retrieved her room key from one of the receptionists, who was waiting for them at the hotel entrance. She started walking toward her room, escorted by a hotel attendant. Suddenly, she felt very dizzy and breathless. She immediately regretted not taking the prescribed altitude medication; she thought she did not need it. She arrived at the room and took the medication immediately. Cusco is at an elevation of 11,000 feet; therefore, she knew she had to take the medication following her dizzy spell. The travel agency physician, traveling with the group, stopped by to see if she was all right. After a short rest, she ate a light dinner with a few of the trip guests in the hotel. Lying in the comfortable bed ready for a night's rest, Ellie willed herself to be better tomorrow. Because of her physical reaction to the altitude that evening, Ellie planned to adjust her activity pace the next day. The last thing she remembered before she drifted off to sleep was her appreciation for the hotel; they gave each guest a gift to remind them of their visit. The gift for female travelers was a beautiful shawl made with alpaca wool.

After a wonderful breakfast, which provided the

energy they would need for the day, the group headed out for a walking tour of Cusco. Their hotel, built around the remains of Pachacuti's palace, was built in the early 1400s. He was the Inca chieftain responsible for uniting all the tribes in the area known today as Peru. Ellie had read all the books recommended by the travel agency to prepare travelers for the trip. She loved learning and history, so she enjoyed reading the books. Next to the palace was an Inca temple that was still functional. They walked among vendors at the market square and up an endless stairway to stroll among the mountain terraces where food was grown, and alpacas grazed. Still adjusting to the altitude, Ellie did not participate in the afternoon excursion to Saqsaywaman. Instead, she joined a couple of other women in the group for tea and cake in the hotel lobby.

The next morning, the group went to Machu Picchu, which is on a mountain at almost 8,000 feet. Traveling the first leg of this short trip and traversing the mountains was accomplished in a quaint steam engine train. At the end of the line, the group traveled by bus and exited the bus at the base of Machu Picchu. Many believe Machu Picchu honors the Incan sun god Inti. Pictures of this architectural feat pale in comparison to seeing it in person. It was a picturesque and breathtaking view. Many wise people of various career pursuits cannot agree on how this city was built at this altitude, exhibiting structures that would require advanced technology today. It was a dwelling place, a spiritual site, and an agricultural site for many years. For reasons archaeologists have not explained, the people abandoned this city. Ellie would remember this as the most memorable sight on the trip, perhaps because so many mysteries surround its existence. On the way back to the hotel in Cusco, the group rode the same train; soon, after a few cocktails, it became a party train. It did not take long for this transformation at such high altitudes.

About 2,500 miles west of the coast of Peru lies the extremely isolated Easter Island, the eastern point of the Polynesian Triangle. This island presented another opportunity for speculation about the origin of the population, its decline, and the Moai monoliths facing inward to the island, which, according to folklore, protect the island. Still, no one knows from whom or what the island is protected. After landing at the small airport, the group traveled by bus to the hotel where they lodged for a couple of nights. Dinner had a Polynesian flair, and it was light but filling. Local dancers, who exhibited expertise in native Rapa Nui dances, provided the entertainment. Ellie thought the music and movement of the performers were angry and determined rather than joyful, as one would expect. Maybe she was just tired. Her unsettled mood persisted the next morning as she gazed upon the view from the patio. A perfect view of the ocean eased her mood. The group spent the day visiting various historical sites on the small island under a gray sky and a calm, lingering mist that drifted in overnight. The parka she had packed was a lifesaver. The group continued despite the weather, and all agreed that the stop on this isolated piece of land was well worth it.

The energetic, positive American Samoa, located near the center of the triangle, was the opposite of Easter Island. The people were friendly, family-oriented, and industrious, demonstrating how they made different items from the humble coconut tree—furniture, clothing, homes, food, and much more. The entertainment during dinner revealed a sense of happiness in the dancing, a more relaxing enjoyment of life, and a distinctly different tone than the entertainment on Easter Island. This Polynesia was the energetic place that Ellie was familiar with. She sensed a shift in the group's energy during the visit to Samoa. Her only regret was not buying and shipping home a coconut tree leaf rug from the community of women who spent their lives making household items from the plant, mainly for tourists.

Flying across the international dateline, the plane, filled with energetic passengers, headed toward Australia, one of many places on Ellie's travel bucket list. Of course, due to the country's size, the excursion was limited to a small portion of the northern coast, near Cairns. Lodging consisted of a small apartment, much roomier than the hotel rooms she had occupied over the past few days. It even had a washer and dryer; the group took advantage of this and did laundry, knowing this may be the last opportunity to do so (and it was). During dinner the first night, a young woman brought in a cute, cuddly koala bear to visit with the guests. It was a big hit. The next day would be long as they headed toward the Great Barrier Reef. First, the group boarded a mini-submarine that enabled everyone to see the reef underwater. It was beautiful; however, not as beautiful as it was a few years ago. The ocean's temperature increased a fraction of a degree, upsetting the ecosystem and killing the reef. It would be a tragedy if that extraordinary reef ceased to exist. Next, those who wanted to snorkel the reef were provided the appropriate gear and paddled into the ocean to see the reef. Ellie declined but had fun watching everyone who did. The last day, the group visited a national game reserve where they observed native animals, including kangaroos, wallabies, and other animals; there was also time for shopping in Cairns. Australia was still on Ellie's bucket list. There was so much there to explore.

Cambodia was the next stop on the itinerary, with Angkor Wat as the highlight. Ellie had seen documentaries on this ancient temple and grounds. She had become fascinated with this historic and spiritual site and Buddhism, a religion that interested her. The hotel was modern and comfortable, with notable attention to detail from the staff. The restaurant was a first-class establishment, and the food satisfied their craving for authentic Asian food. Ellie enjoyed the latter as room service on the first night, as they had arrived late, and she was tired. Following a hearty breakfast the next morning, the group boarded a small bus to Angkor Wat. The weather was beastly, with a temperature of 95 degrees and equal humidity. Everyone began shedding their jackets as soon as they stepped off the bus. Fortunately, the guide walked slowly to prevent overexerting the group. The site was a Buddhist temple surrounded by a high wall. Buddhist monks were still using the temple; a small gathering of monks worshipped as the tour group silently observed the detailed carvings in the stone walls. The structure has a subterranean system that prevents flooding. Excavations surrounding the site revealed that thousands of people, the Khmer, lived outside the temple wall hundreds of years ago. After two hours of climbing steps and walking the trails throughout the site, the group was drenched in sweat and ready to board the air-conditioned bus. They toured two other temple ruin sites as they returned to the hotel. They were much smaller than Angkor Wat.

That evening, the group enjoyed a special event: dinner under the stars and entertainment on the grounds of the ruins of another temple. They arrived at dusk, but torches and small lights lit up the grounds and dining area. Each window of the temple contained a light. The whole area looked like a movie set. Soft music began playing as the group waited for their food to arrive. The first piece was a piano and violin rendition of "Unchained Melody," Lundy's favorite song. Ellie immersed herself in a different dimension, listening to the music and feeling his presence. During dinner, Khmer dancers entertained them. Their performance was hypnotic, unlike anything Ellie had seen before. The meal was fantastic and included a unique presentation of seven miniature desserts. It is a good thing the trip was physically active because the group was enjoying way too many calories.

The next day, the group traveled to a location on the Siem Reap River that contained a village of approximately 10,000 Vietnamese inhabitants living in homes and operating businesses along the river. The Vietnamese village had churches, bars, houses, stores, and other businesses one would find in a grounded village. Cambodia would remain Ellie's favorite place. She felt the presence of Lundy there.

The airport in Kathmandu, Nepal, lacked adequate infrastructure and modern efficiencies. It was a foretaste of what lay ahead when the group meandered through the streets of Kathmandu on a bus. Nepal is in the Himalayas between India and China. The primary religion is Hindu, as evidenced by stupas erected throughout the area. Hinduism was another religion that interested Ellie, not that it was appealing, but because it was polytheistic. Most streets were unpaved with humongous potholes; even the paved portions had potholes. Numerous webs of protruding wires covered the electrical poles. In her journey log, Ellie wrote, "I wonder how AT&T, Comcast, and Spectrum could sort out the mess." She wondered how many power outages the city had each month. Nepal was a step below Cuba.

They ate lunch in the outdoor restaurant after they checked into the hotel. While they enjoyed a delicious meal, including pasta, chicken, and vegetables, the hotel staff delivered their luggage to the rooms. The hotel was an oasis in the middle of chaotic, dirty, crowded Kathmandu. A very high brick wall surrounded the hotel, providing the guests with a sense of security. That afternoon, the group was transported to a tourist shopping area in Kathmandu, where The Little Buddha was filmed. In another area, they observed outdoor cremations along the river, and cows roaming the streets rummaging through trash piles for food. Ellie's room was extravagant, revealing a large bedroom with a king-sized bed and a sitting area upon entry into the room. The bathroom was half the size of the bedroom, with a sunken tub and a walk-in shower. She would have preferred they remain in their rooms for the entire evening, but they had to attend an evening information meeting. The next day, the group split into two groups, each flying to their destination. The larger group flew by jet to Tibet to tour the Potala Palace, where the Dalai Lama had resided before being forced into exile in China in 1970. The other group, Ellie's choice, flew in a smaller propeller-driven plane to Chitwan National Park south of Kathmandu. It was a game preserve dedicated to protecting the white rhinoceros, which was on the verge of extinction, and providing a home for various wildlife.

While all were praying for their lives during the noisy, bumpy ride to Chitwan, the smaller group faced another anxious incident as they attempted to leave the airport. A small group of vehicles, each with two men, surrounded the travelers' vehicles and would not let them pass. The tour guide contacted local officials, who convinced the kidnappers that they would not give them money to allow passage. While the negotiations were ongoing, the tour guide escorted the 12-person group to a nearby hotel room.

They waited for two hours before being allowed to continue on their journey. It was dusk when the group arrived at the lodge where they stayed for a couple of nights. The day had been exciting, to say the least, and they were tired. Ellie decided to forgo the scheduled dinner and entertainment that evening, opting to get a couple of drinks from the bar, go to her room, shower, and go to bed. Ellie did not sleep well that night; her nerves were still on edge from the flight and kidnapping attempt.

The next morning, the group walked to a small area near the lodge to see two elephants receiving a bath. Two large Indian female elephants sauntered to the group, accompanied by their caretaker. Guests were allowed to walk up to the elephants, touch them, ride them, and assist with bathing them. They thoroughly enjoyed this experience and were convinced humans should not let this honorable creature become extinct. They spent the afternoon on a vehicle safari throughout the park, which was covered with dense vegetation, making it hard to see most of the animals. As dusk approached, the group finally saw a white rhinoceros—success. They all enjoyed a wonderful dinner on the patio, watching wildlife by the river behind the lodge. Ellie slept better that night. The next morning, they returned to the small aircraft to fly back to Kathmandu. They passed through small villages and fields where people were manually harvesting rice, a scene that particularly moved her for some reason. As they were waiting to board the plane, the guide told them that the Chinese were detaining the group's plane in Tibet. After the Chitwan group returned to Kathmandu, they had to wait approximately four hours for the group from Tibet because of delays caused by the Chinese. They were all grateful to be back on the British plane; Ellie finally breathed normally, deep and long, after a couple of days of holding her breath.

The group arrived at a modern, efficiently operated Indian Air Force base in Agra, India. It was the first time in days that Ellie felt safe. The group arrived at their palatial hotel after an hour-long bus ride to Agra. Each room had a view of the Taj Mahal. Almost everyone loved dinner; Ellie had never developed a taste for curry and Indian spices, but she consumed the curry-laden food out of politeness. The next day, they toured the Taj Mahal, learning that it was a mausoleum built for the Shah's wife in the 1600s. The tour guide, who spoke English well, was exceptional, cautioning the group not to be taken in by locals who would approach tourists to take their picture for a fee. The group arrived early, hoping to catch the sunlight cast on the granite of the building. Depending on the amount of light and angle of viewing, the granite would appear to be a different color. Unfortunately, the sky was overcast that morning, so the spectacular view did not materialize. However, the sky cleared in the late morning, and the granite color displayed like magic. Reflecting on the tour as the bus returned the travelers to the hotel, Ellie could only think of the following words to describe the site: "The Taj is the most beautiful building I have ever seen." The rest of the afternoon, they shopped in Agra. People mingled everywhere, which did not surprise Ellie since India is the second most populous country in the world. Ellie bought a couple of gifts for friends and a small treasure for herself at a high-end jewelry store. She did not commit to adding India to her travel bucket list, as she had done with Australia.

The flight to Tanzania was long, but the delicious food prepared by the chef and the flight staff en route provided excellent diversions. After they arrived at the Kilimanjaro International Airport, the group boarded minibuses that carried them to their lodging. As dusk fell, the caravan stopped several times to allow migrating herds of wildebeest and zebras to cross the dirt road ahead of the safari vehicle. What an incredible sight to be so close to those beautiful animals. The entire group stayed in the same lodge with isolated cabins built to cater to Westerners who lodged there only to go on a safari through the Serengeti Plain. The lodge managers warned everyone to lock their patio doors and close the exterior blinds when retiring at night, as baboons had managed to get into rooms and scatter guests' items. The managers also warned them that if a baboon did make it into your cabin, do not fight it—"you will lose." The first thing

Ellie did when she entered her cabin was go to the patio and look at the beautiful Serengeti Plain. She instantly felt calm and peaceful; there was an energy here she had never felt before. Soaking in as much of it as possible, she tore herself from the trance to meet the group for dinner and the entertainment afterwards. She successfully secured the cabin against the baboons.

The next day, everyone piled into safari jeeps with cameras for a day of hunting wildlife. Each jeep went in a different direction to prevent scaring the animals with the caravan. The guide/driver in Ellie's small group knew where to find wildlife and explained their habitats and habits as they observed them. The group saw every species of animal one would expect to find in Africa. Her favorite stop was observing a small group of lionesses with their cubs. One cub, mostly hidden in wild grass, was only a few weeks old, but Ellie got a perfect shot of its beautiful little face looking through the prairie grass. They did not see any lions in the group, as they were probably out hunting for food. She had brought a point-and-shoot digital camera specifically for the trip; with a 10x zoom, it made fantastic shots. Weeks after the trip, Ellie compiled her photos and journals for a video, and the only comment she made was, "There are no words to describe the beauty of the Serengeti; just look at the pictures." The excursion to Tanzania elevated visiting other African countries to the top of her bucket list. When the plane departed for Jordan, it flew slightly off course to ensure everyone could see Mount Kilimanjaro close up. The world indeed is beautiful.

Since Ellie had traveled to Saudi Arabia and Israel while on active duty with the military, she knew what to expect when they arrived in Jordan; the group viewed dry, sparsely vegetated desert terrain while riding in a modern, air-conditioned bus from the airport to Wadi Musa, adjacent to Petra. The hotel was nothing spectacular. However, it was modern, plainly decorated, featured running hot and cold water, and a reasonably comfortable bed. This area of the world is not renowned for its spectacular cuisine; Ellie grabbed some snacks and a soda for dinner. The hotel breakfast buffet the next morning was more palatable and Western, which was a good thing, as the rest of the day would be physically challenging.

Centuries ago, Petra was a thriving and prosperous trade center. It was the entrance point into the Middle East for goods from the Orient, especially spices. Petra is a rock-carved city; Tourists can view temple ruins, offices, stores, and various businesses there. Ellie's group could only observe from afar, as they were forbidden to enter the ruins. The first decision Ellie had to make for the day was whether to walk a mile through the Al-Siq Canyon to the city or ride in a donkey-pulled cart. She opted for the donkey cart because the expedition was nearing the end, and her energy level had waned. She and another aging female in the group paired up, and off they went. They passed younger members of their group who were walking and waved arrogantly at them. The road was a dry, clay-filled path with many holes, which quickly ejected the two women and sent them crashing back to the hard seat instantly. The cart ride was very bumpy, and Ellie and her cart buddy did not like how the driver treated the donkey, snapping the leather leads over the back and head of the docile animal. At the end of the cart ride, both women looked at each other and decided they should have walked. And in simple English, they told the driver he should treat his donkey better, and they made their point by hugging the animal's neck.

The Al-Siq opened onto a vast area with the library site directly across the canyon entrance. The library was originally a temple and is the most photographed spot in Petra. The tourists occupied the area, many vendors hawked their wares, and camel owners offered rides through the area. All Ellie could think about was how chaotic everything seemed to be. After all the group members finally assembled with the tour guides, they walked about a mile to view the magnificent architectural feats carved out of the rock. They stopped for lunch at a tourist place where Ellie chose a gyro-like sandwich, thinking it would be safe to eat. After finishing the tour, Ellie had to make another decision—walk or take the cart back. At this point, she was numb, so she and her cart partner chose a cart with a different driver and donkey. Was the way back to the hotel better than the morning trip, or was she just zoned out? She slept well that night.

On day two, they drove to and from and walked part of Wadi Rum, where the movies Lawrence of Arabia and The Martian were filmed. Buses carried the group to the entrance, where they piled into several jeeps. The only vegetation observed was a lone acacia, with roots extending deep in search of water. To their amazement, they walked upon what looked like a Bedouin encampment; however, it was a tourist shop. The travelers browsed around until the owners served them tea in the desert. A little kitten who greeted each traveler as it walked the entire circumference of each table provided the entertainment. The group returned to the hotel after experiencing enough dry, hot desert. The jeep drivers did wheelies in the sand as they raced back to the buses. Her jeep came in third place. Removing all the desert sand from her walking shoes took a long time. Ellie had seen enough of the Middle East; she had no desire to return.

The last stop on the expedition was on the west coast of Africa, Marrakech in Morocco. This Arab imperial city, once a French colony, has embraced Western culture; the French influence was everywhere. Noted for its gardens and irrigation system, it seemed out of place so close to the Sahara Desert. The hotel was grand, modern, and cheerful. Each room overlooked gardens. The next day included a tour of what was once a harem, now a school for young boys studying to be religious leaders, and a tour of the Medina souk. The souk, or market, was crowded with vendors and people purchasing food, spices, clothing, and other wares. The group stopped at a huge spice vendor, where the owner reprimanded one group member for taking a picture of the shop. It took the guide a few minutes to calm things down. Deleting the image from the camera appeased the owner. Ellie did not do much shopping; her interest primarily rested with observing a place she had never experienced. The final dinner on the journey was spectacular. Not only was the food quite good, but the entertainment was amazing, featuring Arabian music and dancers, surpassed only by the Khmer dancers in Cambodia.

The last day of the journey arrived. Awaiting the travelers was a thirteen-hour flight back to Washington, D.C. Most travelers slept most of the way; others remained quietly introspective, their thoughts focused on the trip.

Some departed almost immediately after landing to go home. Ellie had a layover before her flight back to Texas the next day. Those who remained one more night gathered for dinner in the hotel and shared their most memorable moments from the trip. Ellie sensed a sadness that there were no more memories to collect and no more anticipation of what each day would bring. Or maybe that was her perspective. Ellie landed in San Antonio mid-morning the next day. She went home, unpacked, showered, had a little dinner, got into bed, and slept 12 hours before waking. She hibernated for three days, collecting her thoughts and trying to figure out what she would do after this world trip. She had traveled extensively in her seven decades on Earth, but this trip was the epitome of her travel experience. Ellie knew in her mind that there would never be another adventure like this, and it saddened her. But she was grateful that the universe had given her this gift, a gift that very few people would ever receive. She realized how blessed she was. Within six months, her physical health declined drastically, including her vision. Her excursion days were over; she would never see the other countries on her travel bucket list.

Chapter Twenty-Six – A Spiritual Awakening

"Awakening is not changing who you are,
but discarding who you are not."
—Deepak Chopra

Ellie had been comfortable with her religious position as an agnostic from the time that she was a very young woman, leaving her home, parents, and religious indoctrinations and starting her own life. Her years in the military were not conducive to meditation and spiritual reflection; however, she was cognizant of her inner voice, which guided her from time to time. Labeling it intuition, she dismissed these occurrences as something that everyone experienced. After Lundy died, the grieving process presented experiences that she embraced rather than dismissed. As a flip of a switch brings light into a dark room, a switch in Ellie's mind triggered a change in her thinking and perception of experiences, comparable to lifting a veil that hides the light of a candle.

Lundy had one dominant superstition—lucky pennies. Whenever he caught sight of one, he would always pick it up and place it in a mason jar along with others he had collected. Ellie tolerated this habit but never considered it important enough to spend energy reinforcing it herself. About a week after his death, she engaged in her daily routine of walking a few miles when she decided to detour along a very seldom-used path in the neighborhood. Listening to music on her headphones provided a distraction from her misery. She spotted a speck in front of her on the sidewalk and stopped to investigate the sight. To her dismay, she saw a lucky penny. No one ever walked this path. How did this penny get here? She picked it up and placed it in her pocket, thinking of this incident throughout the walk. When she got home, she put the penny in a small leather coin purse without realizing it. The penny would be the first of her many lucky pennies.

A couple of months later, Ellie made an appointment to see an angel psychic, something she would never have done before Lundy's death. Her purpose for the appointment was to seek advice from this person, who had special spiritual energy, regarding a suggestion made by a female friend she worked with. Her friend suggested they become housemates to share expenses and have someone with whom to keep company. The psychic's advice was revealing and accurate; she advised Ellie that the friend was more solicitous than she was about the proposition. Ellie decided not to pursue the friend's suggestion. As she left the appointment, the psychic suggested that Ellie have a sandwich for lunch. Thinking that was a strange statement, but suddenly becoming hungry, Ellie decided to have lunch at one of her favorite places. After consuming her sandwich, she went to the ladies' room to freshen up before running errands. She sat down on the toilet and looked at the floor. Between her feet lay a lucky penny. Now, this was much too bizarre.

Within three weeks of the last incident, Ellie went to the beach alone to rejuvenate her soul since Lundy was no longer a participant in trips to the beach. They always loved going to the beach. The waves carried bad energy to the ocean as they retreated from the shore. She went to the same hotel where they stayed during their getaways. She even stayed in the same beachfront room where they stayed. After arriving, the first thing she did was go to the patio to take in the view of the ocean. As she approached the patio railing, she saw a lucky penny. There was no doubt in her mind that Lundy was communicating with her. During the three years after his death, Ellie would find many lucky pennies. The frequency of the findings diminished over the years.

A week after Ellie moved into the apartment after selling the house, an inexplicable occurrence with the smoke alarm was the turning point in opening up the world of potential boundless encounters with unknown dimensions. One Saturday morning, while she was doing laundry, the smoke alarm in the hallway outside her bedroom began chirping. Sure that the battery needed replacing, Ellie brought out the step ladder and removed the alarm. It continued to chirp. She removed the battery; it continued to chirp. She wrapped the alarm with towels to help stifle the noise and placed it in the second bedroom closet. She could hear a faint chirping throughout the day, and the sound was still strong when she went to bed. Upon awakening Sunday morning, the alarm was silent. On Monday, when she explained the situation to the apartment maintenance crew, they did not explain the bizarre occurrence. Ellie experienced no fear but rather a curiosity for the cause. A couple of years later, when describing the occurrence to someone highly knowledgeable of esoteric phenomena, they explained it was Lundy trying to communicate with her.

Not only did she have the Unchained Melody music experience in Cambodia, but she also had a similar experience while traveling in Cuba. The travel group was on the bus heading for a site when the songs Waiting for a Girl Like You and I Want to Know What Love Is, by the rock music group Foreigner, began playing over the intercom system. They were two of Lundy's and Ellie's favorite songs, and it was the only time the travel group heard music over the bus intercom system. She knew his presence was near.

Ellie was exposed to Native American beliefs that feathers signify a connection to the Creator. As such, they are considered gifts from the sky. Feathers can have different meanings depending on their color. She began finding feathers in her path in unusual places—in the middle of a parking lot with no trees in sight, on the hood of her car parked in the garage, and a black feather on the beach. Considering feathers as a sign that a higher power was protecting and supporting her, she started saving them. After a few years, she had a large plastic bag of different colored feathers. As with the lucky pennies, the frequency of finding feathers diminished. Ellie stopped saving them at some point, but sometimes she still found a feather in her path. She deduced that her mind was healing; she no longer needed a manifested form to reassure her that she was moving forward in the intended path set for her. Her thoughts were no longer black or white, and the impossible became possible.

She frequently recalled one incident to her memory, and each time it happened, Ellie was perplexed and searched for an explanation. She was in the neighborhood grocery store picking up a few items. As she walked down an aisle towards the toothpaste area, she had to stop her cart when a package on a shelf fell to the floor in front of her. No one else was around, so how did the package end up on the floor? She picked it up, placed it on the shelf, and proceeded to the next aisle to her destination. Looking down the aisle toward the toothpaste, she noticed a young man and a young woman, dressed in 1950s clothing, standing a few feet apart in front of the toothpaste. She reached their location, stopped her cart, and as she turned to the shelf to select her item, another young man with long, light brown hair wearing a light-colored long-sleeved shirt and khaki pants and sandals, looked at her, smiled, and said, "That was very nice of you." Ellie smiled back, but rather than verbally responding to him, she thought, "Well, someone had to do it." He smiled at her again. She retrieved the toothpaste and left, completely dazed by the experience. After a few seconds, she turned around and returned to the toothpaste aisle, hoping to see the three of them again. But they were gone.

A few months after the grocery store incident, Ellie experienced another bizarre event. She had arranged to meet a friend to see a late afternoon movie. After she pulled into the parking lot, she drove to an area where she liked to park, close to the movie theater entrance. She passed a middle-aged man who appeared to be working on a motorcycle in the parking lot. She parked, locked the car, and proceeded toward the theater. She didn't hear the motorcycle approach, but suddenly, the man on the motorcycle was behind her car. Since she was early for the feature, she sat in the lobby to wait for her friend. Two men were seated near the table where she was sitting, apparently finishing a pizza. Based on the men's clothes, she associated them with the man on the motorcycle because they all wore biker clothing. One man got up and returned a few minutes later, stopping at her table. He started talking with Ellie about what movie she was there to see. He pointed toward the other man and indicated that he was his son. She looked toward the man to acknowledge him, but could not see his face. The sun shining through the glass windows of the entrance had created a bright halo around his head. All she could see was his shoulder-length hair. Her only thought was, "I am supposed to talk to him." Her past self would have excused herself and departed for the theater. Instead, she continued to respond to his questions. They discovered they were both veterans; he served in Vietnam. He asked her about her genealogy lineage; she answered that she was of primarily Irish descent. When Ellie's friend entered the door, she told him her friend had arrived. He asked her if he could hug her, one veteran to another. She hugged him. She remembered nothing about the movie because her mind was still on her bizarre exchange with the stranger.

After Lundy's death, Ellie had frequent dreams of not being able to get home from work; she would get lost, or some obstacle would block her path. She dreamed about packing for a trip, only to unpack and repack; this scenario repeated many times in the same dream. She had many other dreams centered around similarly disturbing themes. She never tried to self-analyze the meaning of the dreams or conduct research on them; fear of knowing might have prompted this response. However, three dreams occurred only once that provided her comfort and peace.

The first was an out-of-body experience. Ellie was lying in bed when, gently, her body began to rise to the bedroom ceiling and into space. She observed the Earth as she ascended. She reached a place where she saw a wonderful garden filled with flowers, chirping birds, and a stream of water flowing gently beside a white picket fence. Ellie suddenly woke up from sleep at the height of pure joy in this place. The second dream required her to make a decision. She approached a small, narrow bridge arched over a gently flowing stream; on the other side of the bridge, the path forked into two paths, but there was no continuation of the path she was currently walking. Midway over the bridge, she looked to the right and saw a peaceful, beautiful countryside. Looking to the left, she saw a boat drifting down the small river. People were partying noisily; the same gaiety was evident in the small village on the riverbank. Since the path she was on did not continue forward, she had to choose another path to take. She turned to the right. As she turned, she woke from the dream.

In the third dream, Ellie stood outside a building watching a group of people sitting around a table, talking earnestly. One of the people turned toward Ellie; it was Lundy. Filled with sadness and foreboding, she asked, "You are leaving me again, aren't you?" Without speaking, he shook his head, motioning, "Yes." Heartbroken, she did not want to face this loss again. Suddenly, she felt a hand touch her right shoulder. She was not alone. She woke up. Many years later, Ellie knew that these experiences confirmed her "right" decision that there is a power, an energy, and a benevolent Creator, God, who offers unconditional love and comfort during our time on earth. Ellie still never participated in organized religion; if one had to label her leaning, they would label it as spiritual.

Chapter Twenty-Seven - **Mariah**

"When the student is ready, the teacher will appear.
When the student is truly ready,
the teacher will disappear."
—Lao Tzu

Soon after moving into the retirement community, Ellie stopped by the community library to see if the librarian had stocked the shelves with new releases. An older woman resident (much older than her), a volunteer, was reading a magazine article at the checkout desk. Upon glancing at the magazine, photos of crop circles caught her eye. She was interested in this phenomenon and other documented unexplained celestial occurrences. She asked the woman if she was interested in the subject. To Ellie's surprise, the woman responded, "Yes." About that time, the woman's replacement appeared. As the older woman left, she asked Ellie if she wanted to continue the discussion in the sitting area at the back of the library. For the next two hours, Ellie and Mariah discussed crop circles and other esoteric subjects.

A couple of weeks later, there was a knock at Ellie's apartment door. When she opened it, she saw Mariah holding an armload of books. Ellie invited her in, but she declined entry into the apartment. Without revealing the information contained in them, Mariah insisted that Ellie choose one book and later meet to discuss the publication with her. Scanning the titles of the books, one book title drew Ellie's attention, and she chose it. Mariah seemed surprised at the selection, mentioning they would meet later. After a few weeks, Mariah invited Ellie to dinner in the community dining room. Mariah bombarded Ellie with questions. Why did she choose that book? Did she find it difficult to read? Are you comfortable with the Christian basis of the book? Which part of the book did she read first? She went on and on. While Ellie was responding to Mariah's questions regarding Ellie's opinion of the book, she barely ate a bite of the mediocre meal. Because the book was intellectually challenging, Ellie was uncertain whether she understood the author's intent. Mariah was very patient, imparting decades of accrued experience and knowledge she had acquired from her study of the book. Mariah recommended that Ellie read the daily lessons before proceeding to the text. They agreed to meet weekly to assess Ellie's progress and interest in the book. Mariah and this book would change Ellie's life, expand her newly emerging open-minded thinking, and reveal her life's purpose.

Despite their differences in age, upbringing, work experience, child-rearing, and political views, Mariah and Ellie became friends who engaged in many discussions. As Ellie continued her study of the book, she selected other books that Mariah recommended. Mariah, twenty-five years older, had lived a charmed life. Initially, as an only child of wealthy parents, she enjoyed an abundance of parental attention and material possessions. Her brother, born twelve years after her, became a competitor for everything she had received from their parents. Brother and sister were not close at all. He was not receptive to his sister's lack of interest in the traditional Christian faith. He could not understand her reaction to their father's death. She celebrated his life joyfully while he grieved—a further wedge in their relationship. During college, a rare pursuit for a woman in those days, she met her husband just after World War II started. He wanted to fly planes in the war, and she agreed to marry him before he left, a familiar occurrence during the war. He joined the Army Air Corps and flew bombing missions over Germany. Mariah lived with her parents during his absence. Mariah and their infant son greeted him upon his return from the war. He decided to stay in the military. She never had to work to support herself. She had nannies to care for their two sons, adopting one a few years after the birth of their first. They traveled the world on their military assignments.

In mid-life, Mariah began reading about various subjects such as theosophy, esotericism, Eastern religions, and ascended masters. In her pursuit of finding the truth, she lived in an ashram for a while and obtained an audience with a Guru who recommended a book for her to read, as it had a Christian foundation. That book was coincidentally the first book Ellie selected from those presented by Mariah. She made and kept many friends throughout the country with whom she maintained contact to reinforce their common interests. One such person was a woman who lived in Colorado and suffered from macular degeneration. She had received medical attention for her vision from an ophthalmologist who claimed success in stopping the disease using non-traditional approaches to medicine.

Over the years, as she interacted with her, Ellie considered the information obtained from Mariah. She discarded some and held on to some for further pursuit. When Ellie began to explore the teachings of another spiritual leader, Mariah felt slighted and started to question her involvement with another teacher. Ellie did not understand her attitude; she only wanted to read, ask questions, and explore ideas alien to her. She attended numerous nationwide seminars sponsored by the other teacher for about two years. Ellie eventually lost interest in the new teacher as the reality of the price increase for his time arose. She thought a true teacher would not charge for their time. Mariah also resented Ellie's emerging friendship with a non-traditional Christian church member. But that pursuit faded faster than the spiritual leader. It had become apparent that Mariah did not want Ellie to venture out on her pursuit of the truth.

To restore her influence, Mariah said she wanted someone to write her life story and leave it with her family as a memoir after she passed away. Of course, Ellie agreed to do it because she loved writing, and she loved Mariah. The process for accomplishing the endeavor involved their meeting once a week. Ellie recorded the interview sessions. Each session included a combination of Mariah volunteering her thoughts and Ellie posing questions for her to answer. The following week, when they met, Ellie presented a written copy of what transpired the week before for Mariah's review. Mariah edited it and presented her corrections at the next weekly meeting. After they had worked many hours, they completed the document in six months. Ellie experienced frustration when Mariah changed her mind and decided not to include the stories she previously stated she wanted to include. But they both felt it was a rewarding experience. Ellie considered her time working on this project a gift to her teacher. Others had tried this project in the past, but Ellie was the only person who completed the task to Mariah's satisfaction. Mariah distributed thumb drive copies, as well as hard copies, to all the friends and relatives on her list. All were happy with the results and Mariah's gift to them.

Ellie worked on a video project for a strong Southern Baptist neighbor, an activity to which Mariah objected, feeling threatened by organized religion. Ellie became interested in why her neighbor was adamant about practicing her religion. The neighbor discussed parts of the Bible that seemed to pique her interest. Ellie reached a point where her questions became harder for Mariah to answer. Mariah alluded to the end of their relationship because of their differences in religion and spirituality. After pondering the situation for a week, Ellie deduced that the change in attitude was because she was becoming the teacher, no longer the student. She further decided that maybe it was time to no longer serve as a participant in Mariah's life, as painful as it would be; she was merely moving toward the next step in her spiritual evolution, freeing herself from Mariah's consternation. Ellie sent Mariah a card enclosing a short letter that explained her heartfelt decision. Humbly, she expressed that their service to each other was complete. Mariah had given her time, resources, and energy as Ellie's teacher; Ellie had written Mariah's life story.

They did not waste the ten years they spent together; they were two students of the Creator who still had much to learn. Twice after their separation, Ellie received phone calls from Mariah, who could not clearly express her reason for calling. Ellie knew that the once acute mind of her friend was slipping. Within two years, Mariah passed away during the COVID pandemic; there was no memorial. A few months later, as Ellie opened an email, she heard her old friend's voice. Not comprehending how it could have happened, she listened briefly, only to realize it was part of an interview the two shared in writing her life story. Ellie had saved the recording that they had made. How did the recording open at the same time that she opened the email? Mariah had the last word, after all. And Ellie laughed.

The ideas presented in the book that Ellie studied with Mariah for a decade enabled her to understand that there was a different way of looking at the events and experiences that confronted her. She realized that people or things external to her mind could not provide her the peace she wanted and deserved. She was responsible for her actions, words, attitude, and relationships with people. The body is merely a device to communicate right-minded thoughts to others. She will complete her learning when her time on Earth ends, and then she will leave it.

Chapter Twenty-Eight - Leah

"The most beautiful thing we can experience is the mysterious. It is the source of all true art and science."
–Albert Einstein

During the relationship with Mariah, Ellie formed a friendship with another community resident. Initially, the common bond with Leah was a kinship with another military retiree. Their experiences and assignments were very different, and Ellie became interested in some of Leah's ideas and exposure to a part of the military that Ellie was unfamiliar with. She discovered they shared interests in psychics, psychotherapy, remote viewing, and research of Unidentified Aerial Phenomena and celestial travelers.

Leah and Ellie attended lectures on these subjects presented by well-reputed individuals. They attended services in a non-traditional church. They formed relationships with like-minded people. Ellie had a spiritually based experience with Mariah and a scientifically based relationship with Leah. Ellie knew that at some point, she would have to find her view, perhaps a combination of the two approaches to her search for the truth of man's existence. Or maybe she would turn her back on everything she had learned from her teachers. She was questioning everything.

Although drawn to Leah as an information source, Ellie never formed a close personal friendship with her. She never knew why, since they had so many things in common. Nonetheless, Ellie was there for Leah when she remarried, when the newlyweds had an argument, and when the couple divorced after seven years. One bright spot in Leah's life was her little dog, Luna; Ellie cared for him frequently as the couple traveled through the country's national parks and other places.

Luna was a rescue dog that Leah adopted the day before Luna's scheduled euthanasia. He was an old soul, and his parents loved him dearly. When he was diagnosed with bone cancer, they were devastated. Ellie drove Leah and Luna to the veterinarian's office on the day of the euthanasia; Leah's husband drove himself as they were separated pending a divorce. Ellie was dreading this event, remembering her anxiety during the same event with her little dog. Luna encapsulated an intelligent and remarkable understanding of the human being. The veterinarian staff ushered the human family into a special room at the veterinarian's office, furnished like a small sitting room, not a sterile table surrounded by cabinets. Ellie and the two parents were crying quietly, waiting for the veterinarian to enter to complete the process. As they sat there, Luna managed to struggle to his feet. First, he walked over to Leah and looked into her eyes, waiting for her to say her final words. Next, he went to his daddy for the same opportunity to say goodbye. Then, he walked over to Ellie; she looked into his eyes and thanked him for sharing his life with her. Finally, he went over and lay down by Leah on his blanket. Shortly, the doctor came in and administered the medication. Luna was finally pain-free; he was home. The three of them left with red, swollen eyes.

Ellie felt herself withdrawing more and more from Leah. Intuitive Leah reciprocated and, in her words and actions, basically told Ellie to get lost. They both had reached the point where they were no longer uplifting each other. Ellie realized that the relationship's outcome was her fault; unknowingly, she had not been the friend Leah wanted. She saw Leah a few years later at the doctor's office. She felt no animosity, anger, or hurtful thoughts toward Leah or herself. They shared a few pleasant moments to catch up on the past years. When Leah asked how she was doing, Ellie paused for a second, and Leah responded, "You are at peace now, aren't you?" "Yes," Ellie replied.

Chapter Twenty-Nine - **Sight Loss Event 4**

"In healthcare, the experience of the patient is the new marketing."
—David Feinberg

Nine months after the trip around the world, Ellie contacted one of Mariah's friends to discuss her experience with an ophthalmologist located near Dallas who claimed he could halt the progression of macular degeneration. Mariah's friend had participated in the treatment he offered and achieved success. His integrative approach emphasized oxygen therapy, food supplements, and low-voltage electric energy. Since the process worked for Mariah's friend, Ellie also decided to participate. During her next appointment with her retina specialist, Ellie informed him that she was considering consulting a doctor in Dallas to see if he could help her. Her retina specialist was receptive, asking questions about the methodology and risks involved. He told Ellie, "If you have the money, go for it. All I can do is stick you in the eye. I will see you in three months." Reassured that she had his support, she made plans to take a trip to Dallas and spend a week receiving the treatment to halt the advancement of the macular degeneration. There was one problem. She was nervous about driving herself since she did not know what would happen at the end of the week of treatment.

Additionally, since her vision was deteriorating, she was apprehensive about driving in Dallas traffic. As with many problems Ellie had experienced, someone gave her a solution. A community friend stated she would drive her. Ellie agreed, only if there were friends or family in the area with whom the friend could stay for a week. The friend's best friend lived just east of Dallas. Ellie and her friend finalized the plans, and in a couple of weeks, Ellie, without fear, embarked on an unknown, unique medical treatment that was not traditional.

Her friend dropped her off at the hotel recommended by the doctor's clinic. It was close to the clinic, so she took the hotel shuttle to and from the clinic during the week. Many restaurants were nearby, so she did not need to forage for food. The hotel shuttle delivered her to the doctor's clinic on schedule the next day. In her mind, Ellie envisioned leaving at the end of the week, and since her birthday was Thursday, she knew she would be getting a birthday present from the doctor. The first day consisted of filling out forms, meeting the staff who provided her with information about what to expect during the week, undergoing an exam by the doctor, and receiving her first oxygen therapy in a hyperbaric oxygen chamber.

Consisting of three phases, the initial exam was unlike any she had ever received. First, the doctor held a large crystal above her body, tracing it along energy points to determine if the energy was blocked. Ellie understood the importance of energy flow through the body, a concept she had learned through her participation in kundalini yoga for three years. So far, so good. She did not think this process was medical quackery. He determined there was an energy blockage in two areas of her body. He placed a low-level electrical energy-emitting device against the center of her skull to correct that. After a few minutes, he removed the device and used the crystal again to determine whether there had been a change in the two blocked areas. Ellie deduced the device was instrumental in the correction because the energy seemed to flow normally.

The second phase consisted of a thorough eye examination that included reading eye charts, various retinal scans, and an eye examination performed by the doctor. The purpose was to provide a baseline for Ellie's vision capability before the weeklong therapy began. The same exams were conducted on the last day to determine the therapy results. It is important to note that even after the eye injections in the right eye that Ellie had been receiving, she could only read the first line on the eye chart. Her left eye was still 20/20 with the dry condition of macular degeneration. When the doctor asked her if the injections had helped her vision, Ellie responded that she could not answer the question because she did not know what her vision would be like had she not taken the injections.

The third phase was an oral exam. Ellie had always prided herself on her dental health, cleaning her teeth twice a year, undergoing oral surgeries to ensure a better bite, root canals, fillings, and other procedures. Attention to her oral health was a reaction to her childhood and adolescent experiences with dental issues. Her mouth was too small for her teeth, so she had several extractions for proper alignment and growth. Although she did not eat many sweets or drink soda when she was young, she developed many cavities. As an adult, she attributed her challenged oral health to being the genetic recipient of a particular gene, and the fact that for the first twenty years of her life, her source of drinking water was a well. Well water is not the healthiest water to drink. After considering all this, she asked the doctor why she was getting an oral exam. The response surprised her. The doctor informed her that oral infections can block electrical energy from reaching the different eye cells, which rely on electrical current to repair and produce new cells. He gave her a list of dentists who practiced holistic dentistry, suggesting one of them could determine if there were oral infections in her mouth.

The doctor treated her eyes for the rest of the first day with a device much smaller than the one used to align the body's energy points. He showed Ellie how to use the device by connecting it to another one containing two AA batteries. The other device provided the energy source for the eye treatment device, which transmitted healing energy to the eye cells.

Ellie experienced her first hyperbaric oxygen therapy. She had to crawl into a metal tube about eight feet long and three feet in circumference with a window on top. Upon entering, she lay down on the thin padding of the chamber and looked through the window above her head. Somewhat claustrophobic, Ellie kept her eyes closed for the entire thirty-minute session. Oxygen is critical for repairing the body's cells and generating new ones. This therapy provided more oxygen than one person breathes in from the atmosphere.

Ellie spent Tuesday through Thursday performing balance exercises, taking nutritional supplements, eye treatments, and oxygen treatments. On Friday morning, she had one last eye treatment before seeing the doctor for the exit eye exam. It had been a long week, and Ellie wanted the experience to end on a good note, with better eyesight. She got her wish. Not only could she see the large "E" on the eye chart with her impaired right eye, but she could also see the two lines below it. The left eye was still 20/20, and the scan picture showed a positive change in the dry macular degeneration. Now, she was charged with the continuation of the supplements and daily eye treatments using the FDA-approved devices and oxygen treatments. She purchased two eye treatment devices at a high price. She bought a three-month supply of supplements, one of which was an oxygen production enhancer for the body. Her friend picked her up the next morning, and they headed home.

When Ellie saw her retina specialist two weeks later, he was very interested in hearing about the experience. The scans he ordered for the appointment showed improvement in both eyes. Her right eye had changed from wet to dry; her eyesight improved over time until it reached 20/60, and she could still drive a car. The appointments changed from every three to every six months with no injections.

Ellie faithfully performed the daily eye treatments. However, she quit taking the supplements after six months because she did not see any improvement in the lab results produced for visits with her primary care doctor. But she continued to take the oxygen supplements.

Three months after the Dallas trip, she made an appointment with one of the dentists from the list the Dallas doctor had given her. CT scans of her mouth revealed that one tooth with a root canal had an infection. In each area where the dentist removed the wisdom teeth many years ago, there was a bacterial infection in the pocket. During her second trip to the dentist, he treated the sites of all oral infections that could have affected her vision. The dentist extracted the tooth with the root canal and cleaned the wisdom teeth area using cavitation surgery. Instead of surgical stitches, the dentist used a platelet-rich fibrin. It was healed in two days. Before and after the surgical procedures, Ellie received a body massage. She loved this place. Had it not been an hour's drive from her house, she would have switched dentists. But, again, all the dental work she received came at a heavy cost.

Ellie participated in non-traditional medical processes and procedures; she met the challenges with curiosity, faith, and hope, but not fear. She began focusing on the present moment rather than dwelling on the past or planning for a future that may never happen. She was starting to feel free again.

Part IV: The Time Has Come

Chapter Thirty - The Body Rebels

"She made broken look beautiful and strong look invincible."
—Ariana Dancu

A couple of weeks after the oral surgery, Ellie could hear her inner voice gently speaking as she put on her walking shoes, preparing for a three-mile walk. She attempted to complete a three-mile walk every two days. "The time has come." Vocalizing a response, she responded to the quietness in her bedroom, "For what?" There was no internal response. Throughout the walk, she pondered the meaning of her thoughts; one moment, she felt joy at the anticipated peace and happiness, and the next, she dreaded the adversity that may lie ahead. By the end of the walk, Ellie knew it was time for her to decide how to respond to the events that awaited her with fear or courage. And she knew at that moment she would spend the rest of her life attending to various health issues. She prayed for courage. This walk was her last three-mile walk.

Within a few days of the last three-mile walk, the skin on the bottom of her feet and palms of her hands began to thicken with red, itchy, burning patches. After one week, the skin had become so thick that it started to crack, making walking and handling things difficult. After over-the-counter ointments and creams failed to alleviate the condition, she consulted a podiatrist, hoping he could diagnose the problem and prescribe a solution. The podiatrist informed her that it was a skin condition caused by aging. His solution was to scrape off the thick skin with a scalpel. She applied lotions to her feet and hands and wore socks daily and at night. She wore gloves at night to retain the ointment on the skin. A second trip to the podiatrist resulted in another scraping, drawing blood in one area. She decided he was a quack and considered reporting him to the state medical board. But she had no energy for that now; she had to find someone to help her.

She went to see her new primary care provider, a young doctor who had recently completed residency training. When she first saw him, she asked him how old he was, as he looked like he was still in medical school. But he was eager to ascertain what was going on with her appendages. After ordering lab work, he deduced that Ellie had palm and plantar psoriasis, an autoimmune disorder. She discovered through online research that autoimmune diseases frequently occur in aging populations. The doctor prescribed topical ointments for the feet and hands. When the lab work results came back, he informed her that her thyroid level was too low, which was causing fatigue and weight gain. He changed her medication. Weeks passed, and her body still did not respond to his solutions. He referred her to an endocrinologist to fix the thyroid, which now had an elevated reading, causing hair loss and agitation. She was not sleeping well. He recommended a dermatologist to treat her psoriasis. The fluctuation of thyroid function was creating cardiovascular issues—palpitations, rapid pulse, and increased hypertension. One night, she couldn't sleep because she could feel her heart beating, and her pulse was racing. On the verge of calling an ambulance, Ellie tried meditation, which seemed to work. She was not doing well at all.

It took Ellie three months to get an appointment with the endocrinologist. After presenting a hard copy of the chronology of events over the last months, he said something to the effect of, "We did this to you." He changed her medication. In one year, the thyroid level had stabilized, and her hair was beginning to grow back. Her cardiovascular issues had stabilized.

The dermatologist prescribed a biologic medication, a pill with many side effects, and topical ointments for her feet and hands. The doctor insisted that Ellie take the medication despite Ellie's objections to the side effects. The doctor stood firm. Ellie found a new dermatologist. The new doctor prescribed a different biologic medication with similar side effects to the first medication.

Meanwhile, she continued applying the topical ointments and wearing socks for almost two years.

Not comfortable with her primary care doctor, who began to let his assistant handle her appointments, Ellie deduced that he was tired of trying to help her. She found a new primary care doctor, whom a neighbor recommended. She presented a hard copy of her medical history during the new patient appointment. She liked him immediately; a doctor-patient chemistry was evident. He ordered lab work, referred her to another dermatologist, changed her blood pressure medication, and instructed her to continue seeing the endocrinologist. The lab work revealed abnormal levels for almost all the tests. Ellie and her new doctor began the work needed to bring her body back to life.

The third and final dermatologist was young, competent, and listened to Ellie. After the new patient appointment, Ellie left with different topical medication prescriptions. She had informed the doctor that she did not want to take a medication with as many side effects as were present in the biologics. Socks and gloves remained a part of her clothing attire. After approximately 18 months, her feet and hands had improved significantly, so she no longer needed the topical medications. The doctor asked her how she was feeling otherwise. Ellie explained that her hip joints sometimes locked up, and walking became more strained. The doctor then informed Ellie that she now had psoriatic arthritis and recommended a biologic medication by injection that would target the affected areas of the body instead of shutting down the whole immune system like most medications on the market. By this time, Ellie was confident the advice was sound and agreed. The effects of the medication were so positive that, within six months, Ellie could stand and walk better, and the pain had decreased, producing sounder sleep. Unfortunately, she and the medication would be in a lifelong partnership. The medication could not heal the arthritis, but it made living with it easier. And the medication was costly, resulting in non-payment from the insurance company. Now, Ellie would have to form a partnership with the medication for life and find a way to pay for it without exhausting her funds. Fortunately, the pharmaceutical company that produced the medication approved her application for financial assistance; however, it would be reviewed on an annual basis. What would she do if they no longer funded the medication?

During all this time, she acquired a rare dental disorder known as tooth resorption, an autoimmune condition where the tooth begins to "eat" itself from the inside out. After three months of treatments, the endodontist had repaired the tooth, but the condition reappeared a year later. Because the affected area was well below the gum line, Ellie was required to visit a periodontist to repair it. One might just say, pull the tooth and put in an implant. However, that tooth had the front end of a bridge mounted on it. Losing the tooth would mean removing the whole bridge. The periodontist was able to save the tooth. But with her autoimmune condition, Ellie hoped another tooth would not be affected.

As if all this body rebellion was not enough, her primary care doctor diagnosed atrial fibrillation (AFIB). Off she went to the referred cardiologist, who confirmed the diagnosis after a stress test and various scans. But she lucked out, as she did not require a pacemaker or watchman, just blood thinners for the rest of her life. And she needed to visit him every six months.

Managing her health issues was a full-time effort for five years, and that period of her life was a blur during its existence. It was the focus of her life. A cure did not exist for the autoimmune disease, so she would have to take lifelong medication for the arthritis. She would be on a blood thinner for the rest of her life. Hopefully, no other cardiological disorders would erupt. If nothing else went wrong with her body, Ellie reconciled herself to managing her life with maintenance medications from the various doctors. So far, she had faced it all with courage. Her vision was a different story; still, another situation would arise, requiring the most courage her spirit could muster.

Chapter Thirty-One
- A Change is Needed

"A change is as good as a rest."
—Stephen King

After living in the retirement community for over twelve years, Ellie realized it was time for her to move for several reasons. She finally realized that fear caused her to move from the apartment to the community, an emotion she thought was nonexistent. She was in her sixties then, with no family and few friends to count on in her time of need. A retirement community afforded her physical safety, a staff charged with taking care of her physical needs (food, shelter, maintenance of the dwelling, recreation, transportation to medical appointments, etc.), physical and mental health when needed, and religious needs if so inclined. Located in a quiet neighborhood outside the city, the community offered a more relaxed atmosphere free from the hustle and bustle of city traffic.

Ellie developed a few friendships with some of the

residents over the years, but none of the relationships were strong and lasting or founded on mutual respect and interests. Perhaps the relationships were formed based on her perception that she needed someone other than herself for happiness and to find someone to fill a void within herself. She realized that relying on others to make her happy was an illusion. Wasn't that true for all the relationships she had experienced? She was happy with Lundy but wasn't looking for anything from him when they met, and she never wanted anything from him. They mutually gave to each other and lifted each other—the holy relationship with him did this.

The fact that the residents were either retired military officers or spouses of such was initially a positive factor in deciding to move there. They all came from the same career orientation, shared similar experiences, were stationed in the same location, and were successful. As the years went by, this factor became less important to her. The residents were proud of their service to the country, and so was Ellie. She felt genuinely honored to belong to such a patriotic population that put their interests second to those of the country. But that was a former life, at least in her mind. She had begun to change in many ways while still supporting the Constitution of the United States. She no longer fit in. Focused on the present and not the past, she wanted to meet and get to know people from different career paths with varied interests. She wanted to hear different life stories and learn from them; in the back of her mind, she desired to find another soul who would lift her up and walk the spiritual path with her, knowing the odds of this success would be very slim. If it happened, that would be a blessing; if it did not, she was prepared to proceed down the path alone, accompanied only by her Creator.

There were other factors involved in her decision to move. The once quiet, peaceful neighborhoods surrounding the community had rapidly grown, resulting in one of the highest crime areas in the county. Security was beginning to become an issue in some areas of the community. Community management was experiencing staff personnel issues and confronted a facility aging dilemma that could impact future occupancy rates. Ellie loved her yard surrounding the duplex where she resided; it was the envy of the neighborhood. But she was older now, and her energy level had diminished as a result of all her health issues. She could no longer, nor wanted to give it any more attention. Without telling her neighbors or friends, she submitted her notice to vacate her home in 90 days. Eventually, word did get out regarding her decision to leave. Now, she had to find another place to live. She knew just where to look.

Chapter Thirty-Two - **Quest to Find A New Abode**

"Home isn't where you're from, it's where you find light when all goes dark."
—Pierce Brown

After touring several retirement communities to find a potential new home, Ellie chose one in a part of the city that came to mind first. It was a well-established, eclectic part of town; everyone who could afford it moved there. The crime rate was almost nonexistent due to a highly effective police department, stores offering various products, and upscale restaurants located within a mile of her new home. The retirement community was a 1970s structure; through the 1990s, it was considered the best place to retire in the city. When she toured the interior, she felt a twinge of disappointment that it reminded her of an old folks' home. The facility needed upgrades badly; she sensed that the deferred maintenance was the norm, just as it had been where she previously resided. However, they had an apartment of the size that she wanted. As an incentive, management gave her two months of free rent. Despite a nagging reluctance, she believed she would make it work. After all, the location was ideal. She signed a one-year lease.

Within a month, Ellie was in her new home, snug but comfortable. The view from the patio was nice, but a little noisy due to the nearby traffic, which was only a mile away. Although it was close to the airport, there was no airplane noise disturbance. After a week of being awakened each morning due to the commuting traffic on the freeway, she had become a little irritable. She complained about the noise and disruption to her sleep, which brought a commitment from management to upgrade the bedroom windows. Another strange phenomenon that occurred frequently early in the morning was that her TV would mysteriously turn on, although she had not turned it on. A second complaint produced no resolution from management. The dishwasher broke; a water line from the kitchen sink started leaking, damaging property in the apartment below her; the refrigerator needed replacing; and the final straw was that the water consistently was not hot for six months. When she left the community at the end of the year's lease, the water issue still had not been fixed. Ellie was upset with herself because she hadn't listened to her inner voice. She had made a bad decision.

In addition to all the physical faults with the facility, the residents were not friendly. They were proud that they had lived their whole lives in this part of town and were descendants of "so and so who did this and that." So much for being around different people to learn about various things.

The Universe took care of Ellie, though. A few blocks away was a retirement community only eight years old. She did not include it on her original list to visit because a friend had told her it was too expensive. Her friend provided this information to Ellie after she had considered moving there herself. Ellie trusted the friend's advice. After touring the new facility, she was delighted. It was in the area she wanted to live. Yes, it was more expensive, but it was a newer establishment, and she would have hot water. She loved her spacious apartment; the residents were nicer, there were more activities, and she felt safer. She lived in this apartment for a few years until she was declared officially blind on her 80th birthday. Due to government law, all persons with disabilities had to relocate to special facilities that could meet their specific needs.

Chapter Thirty-Three - **Sight Loss Event 5**

"Don't cry because it's over,
smile because it happened."
—Dr. Seuss

At age 77, Ellie's faithful retina specialist informed her that the macular degeneration in both eyes had progressed to the advanced form known as GA (geographic atrophy). Her central vision would be gone within five years, leaving only peripheral vision. Medication did not exist to stop its progression at this time. Only one eye injection medication existed, but it would only slow the progression of her vision loss. One side effect of the medication was total blindness. The blindness ratio was 1:4500 for those who had chosen the injection, which was not good odds. Ellie declined the medication. Her doctor supported her decision. The time had come to plan how she would compensate for the complete loss of her central vision.

Unable to see well enough to navigate the airport

requirements and refusing to be a burden to a travel companion, Ellie decided to cancel a cruise through the Panama Canal, hoping she could take one final trip. She felt that her vision could worsen when the time came to take the cruise, which would affect sightseeing and pose challenges at the airport. She knew that her travel days were over, at least those that required air travel. Ellie could still manage road trips if she had someone to drive; however, no one was willing or able to serve as her driver on a road trip. She decided to cancel all future travel plans. For a short while, she mourned the loss of an experience that meant so much to her—to see the world's wonders afforded by travel. Ellie stopped feeling sorry for herself and thanked her Creator for all that she had been able to see during her lifetime—far more than most people could imagine.

Chapter Thirty-Four - Sight Loss Event 6

"I have never been disabled in my dreams."
—Christopher Reeve

Ellie celebrated her 80th birthday by attending an appointment with her retina specialist. She had quit driving five or six years ago because of her vision. She relied on the transportation service provided by the retirement community to get her to and from various medical appointments. At this stage in her vision deterioration, she could see no improvement at all. However, the situation could worsen depending on the allergens in the air, her lack of sleep, or her blood pressure. When she watched TV, she saw blurred images, and she couldn't see the faces of the people appearing on the screen. Using her peripheral vision was tedious and very time-consuming, most often resulting in severe headaches.

She could tell something was not right when the doctor walked into the examination room, and he did not greet her with, "Hello, beautiful." Bracing for a setback, she stated, "Let's have it." He informed her that she was now legally blind. If one is determined to be legally blind, that person is considered disabled. Knowing this day would eventually come, she was not sad or surprised by the news. She was grateful for the time she had spent with sight. She was confident that she had contributed positively to her life and the path planned for her. She dreaded what the doctor would say next; it would mean a significant change in her life, over which she had no control, and she could not yet assess how she would compensate for the disability. He emphasized that he was required to report the disability to the government authorities. She responded by shaking her head and saying, "Yes." Ellie rose from the chair, shook his hand, thanked him for all his help through the years, and walked out of his office for the last time.

Chapter Thirty-Five - The Final Move

"Just when I think I have learned t he way to live, life changes."
—Hugh Prather

During the last forty to fifty years of Ellie's life, changes impacting the planet's inhabitants occurred with accelerated intensity. The simultaneous convergence of changes in cosmological, planetary, species evolution, technology, geopolitical, and extraterrestrial influences became overwhelming. Any semblance of effective leadership, at any level of government, required to implement and enforce positive, moral, and common-sense actions, had eroded. In her advanced years, Ellie had accumulated experience and wisdom sufficient to view the turmoil and discern that it was all perfectly natural in the planet's total evolution. Everything was aligned as it should be according to Divine will. Losing her central vision was a blessing at this point, as she could no longer see all the changes through the eyes of her body.

Solar storms had increased and occurred more frequently, penetrating and weakening the Earth's magnetosphere, which consequently affected the planet's habitability. Forests began to die off due to decreased oxygen in the air, and the mortality of people with respiratory health issues increased. The warmer ocean temperature resulted in a massive loss of sea life, an essential component of the human food chain. An increase in energy waves was bombarding the atmosphere and the planet's surface, ranging in length from the longest form of X-rays to the shortest form of gamma rays, resulting in increased outages of global communication systems and increases in radiation-related health conditions. Although it would be six billion years before the sun enlarged to engulf the planets Mercury, Venus, and Earth, current solar flare activity could devastate the planet.

As the average global temperature increased annually, ocean water levels began to rise, affecting coastal communities and habitats. Hurricanes increased in number and intensity; therefore, coastal communities ceased to exist. Wildfires increased in frequency and size, destroying populated areas and national forests, creating a void in watersheds that resulted in flooding nationwide. Global earthquakes increased in number and severity. Scientists predicted the Earth would collide with an asteroid in three years. Potential damage to the plant was unknown, or at least global leadership did not inform the population of the possible risks. Although the United States successfully landed a spacecraft with a crew on Mars, the human race could not inhabit the planet if an extinction event destroyed the Earth.

All industrialized nations globally experienced a

decline in their birth rates, resulting in a decreased workforce, which was corrected only by massive immigration from other overpopulated, underdeveloped countries. This accepted practice led to the general degradation of human services provided to the population. The world could no longer effectively protect borders between countries; consequently, legal immigration enforcement ceased. Diverse cultures competing for the same resources and services produced astronomical increases in crime in urban and rural areas. Law enforcement became virtually ineffective. In the United States, local law enforcement agencies merged with federal law enforcement to form the national police force, which was responsible for enforcing the laws of the land. Corruption among the ranks left the population vulnerable.

Farmlands were abandoned or rendered unproductive due to drought and erratic weather patterns; food was scarce and expensive. Education systems became overwhelmed, failing to graduate young people who could read, write, or demonstrate acceptable math skills that were once the country's pride. They possessed minimal information and skills needed to become productive citizens. They were extremely proficient with computer technology but not accomplished in verbal communication skills. Children could no longer perform at the designated level instituted ten to fifteen years prior. Institutions of higher learning were producing graduates with diplomas that equated to high school graduates ten years ago. With the nationalization of healthcare came a decline in the quantity and quality of healthcare services. As hospitals closed, the mortality rate increased. Of particular concern to Ellie was care for the aging population.

The government threw the aging population, who had no family to take them in or lacked financial resources, into government-financed and operated nursing care or assisted living facilities. The frequency of changes to laws increased rapidly until the weight of adapting to them became impossible for the average person.

Competition for resources caused global skirmishes among neighboring countries and threats of nuclear war among the most powerful nations. The structure of the national government, a republic, as cited in the Declaration of Independence, dissolved due to the corruption of all branches of the government. No leaders stepped forward to reverse the decline. The major political parties ceased to exist because of a unification of ideology, further corrupting the government. Seven leaders representing finance, business, manufacturing, technology, defense, healthcare, and agriculture stepped forward to form an oligarchy to provide some semblance of order to save the country. Covertly organized, the group of seven persuaded the military to join them in overthrowing the existing incompetent government. These leaders were still in the process of organizing their subordinate organizations and delineating responsibilities. The media reported directly to the group through one person selected by the media front. Ellie thought the emerging global situation was pure chaos that no human being could calm; peace to the planet required a higher source of intelligence and order.

Ellie was somewhat isolated in her retirement community. She was bombarded daily with the media, which represented the oligarchy's interests and provided citizens with information (orders) deemed appropriate by the group. Her retirement community had reduced the meals to one meal per day and decreased the portion sizes, while the resident deaths increased. The community had not experienced any security breaches; however, a gang of young men searching for money or food breached the neighboring retirement communities. Ellie tried not to become entangled in the world's ways; instead, she maintained an open mind and let her instinctive thoughts guide her to a position she discerned as the right-minded one.

One afternoon, while watching television, Ellie was interrupted by a knock on her door. She could not imagine who it could be since few people had visited her anymore. People generally did not venture out much, let alone visit other people. When she opened the door, a young woman warmly greeted her and introduced herself as a case worker for the National Relocation Service. Ellie invited her into the apartment, apologizing for having nothing to offer her to eat or drink except water. Getting right to the point of the visit, the young woman informed Ellie that her office had received a notification from her retina specialist reporting that she was now legally blind. Therefore, within two months, Ellie would be relocated to a facility that provided housing and food for people disabled due to blindness. The young woman showed Ellie a brochure containing a picture of the facility and explained their services. It was much smaller than her current place, so Ellie immediately thought about what household items she could move. After downsizing many times over the years, she had little left. Now, a further reduction in her material possessions awaited her.

Chapter Thirty-Six
- The Final Home

"Our homes are not defined by geography or one particular location, but by memories, events, people, and spaces that span the globe."
—Marilyn Gardner

Ellie's few friends at the retirement community expressed concern for the government-dictated move and wished her well. Ellie told them to spread the word that she planned to give away some items; anyone interested had two months to retrieve them. Within a month, she had given away most of her belongings. Giving away material possessions had never been a difficult chore for her; it was just stuff she had procured, thinking they would fulfill a need, emotional or physical. Her remaining possessions included one reclining chair partnered with a side table and table lamp, one serving tray to serve as a table for her meals, one standard reclining hospital bed accompanied by one nightstand and table lamp, one desk with chair, and a television with a cabinet—she could still see some objects through her peripheral division, but no faces or words and, of course, she still could hear. A small closet could accommodate her clothing items. She gave most of her clothing away. She no longer needed multiple clothing items or colorful outfits—she would have no place to go.

These few items would fit comfortably within the 600-square-foot apartment of her final home. She would have no kitchen or dining area, just a microwave on a small cabinet and a mini refrigerator. There was room for only one tableware setting and utensils in the small cabinet. The facility would serve her one meal each day. Since she could no longer read, there would be no books, which in the days of vision provided a meaningful escape from the world's illusion that her eyes saw. She would retain her mobile phone and download audiobooks to enjoy, although she preferred keeping her sight and reading ability. Her phone was a new technology produced for the visually impaired. It contained raised letters or numbers similar to Braille, accompanied by audio assistance. The television remote had a similar capability.

Two months and one week after the visit from the National Relocation Service case worker, two men showed up at Ellie's apartment in mid-morning to relocate her to the facility housing the visually disabled residents. In less than an hour, the relocation service had removed Ellie's belongings from her retirement community apartment. Simultaneously, with the departure of the moving team, the case worker reappeared, this time to transport Ellie to her final home. She explained to Ellie that 10 facilities throughout the country housed the visually disabled residents. Ellie was lucky; her home would be in Texas, in the Midland-Odessa area, about five and one-half hours northwest. They spared no time departing for the relatively short trip. She was grateful to have company for a while, but disappointed that she could not enjoy the scenery of the Basin and Range Province of Texas. Ellie was never very talkative, but she was an excellent listener. She had a few hours to pry as much information as possible from the young woman about the country's current political and social climate, hoping for accuracy unfiltered by the media. Maybe a mid-level government employee would be willing to share what she knew with an elderly woman who had no one to gossip with and probably had only days left to see the sun rise each morning.

Attempting to build trust with the young woman, Ellie began a slowly paced conversation centered on the young woman. She grilled her on the following: "Are you married? Do you have Children? Tell me about them. Where did you go to school? Did you receive a college degree? What was your major? Are your parents still alive? What about siblings? What do you like about your job? What do you dislike about your job? What are your hobbies?" When they stopped for a quick lunch, Ellie felt she could raise the conversation level to suit her interests.

With minimal dining options along the route thus far, they passed a local Mexican restaurant with potential. Both decided it would be best to turn around, as they may not find anything better ahead. Ellie had not eaten in a restaurant in a very long time. She was amazed that the menu items were minimal now, with only one page of selections, which were all specials. The menu had no regular items. She loved fish tacos and immediately ordered them. Unfortunately, they had no fish. They did not have chicken either. So, she ordered the beef tacos, although she anticipated she would not feel well after the meal since she had not eaten beef in twenty years. The rice was delicious, and so were the Borracho beans. Since this meal was on the government, Ellie also ordered flan for dessert. The restaurant did not have a bar, so she could not order a margarita. Bottled water was her beverage choice. Ellie and the young caseworker did not talk much during lunch. Both were hungry and spent their time feeding their faces. While the young woman filled the car with fuel, Ellie prepared herself for the next round of questioning, which proved fruitful for her.

The national military structure had tripled in size, yet the nation was not fighting a kinetic war or conflict of any kind; however, the threat of such an event was constantly looming with several nations. The government used one-third of the force to back up the national police force during daily riots throughout the country. The population was rioting about human rights violations under the Constitution, which was in the process of being amended to eliminate many of the original rights. People rioted about food and fuel shortages, travel restrictions, wealth redistribution, mandatory relocations, inflation, low wages, etc. The news media didn't inform the public of events occurring globally. The global population was starving for truthful information, which would not be forthcoming due to the eradication of social media outlets.

Care for the elderly and disabled people was draining financial and personnel resources from other governmental interests. To create more efficiency and cost savings, the government established care communities for all disabled people. The government established separate communities for the blind, deaf, immobile, persons with mental and cognitive disorders, and those in the population with chronic disabling diseases. They transferred the affected persons into these facilities; they had a four-month turnover. Even the young caseworker did not know the disposition of the disabled community residents. Only personnel three steps above her pay grade were privy to that information. Baseless gossip among the National Relocation Service staff produced several speculations. They were sent to assisted living or nursing facilities, maybe to a different country. Other sources reported using floating cities that traversed global coastlines. They docked in locations with the resources to support the disabled people. There were stories of sending them to another planet in an Unexplained Aerial Phenomenon space craft. Some died naturally, by their own hands, or with assistance from the care staff. Only a few managers at ultra-high-level government oversight offices knew what happened to the disabled people after four months of resettlement into the communities.

The sun was beginning to set when they arrived at the disabled community for the blind where Ellie would reside. She thought of the many sunsets she had witnessed in her life. The most memorable were the ones with the sun slipping into darkness over a vast ocean. The facility included hastily erected, concrete and steel modules. It was cold and uninviting. No vegetation sprang from Midland's dry, desert soil; there was no visible attempt to grow vegetation. What was the point since people coming here were blind in some form? At least Ellie still had peripheral vision.

The empty apartment was as nondescript as the exterior of the building; Ellie would have to humanize it with the few belongings that would arrive any minute. Contrary to her experience with government employees for most of her life, the government efficiently executed this move. The two men who picked up her belongings arrived and placed the meager belongings Ellie had selected in position as she instructed. The case worker informed her that a different case worker would meet with her in a few days. She gave Ellie an emergency contact number before she left Ellie's apartment. Within an hour, all team members were gone; Ellie was alone. Her food would be delivered twice daily, one more meal than usual. Maybe they were trying to fatten her up. A few minutes later, a small Asian female who spoke little English delivered her evening meal. In broken English, she told Ellie to leave the tray outside the door when finished. She soon learned that food choices were not an option; one could eat what they offered or choose not to eat. She was tired and hungry the first night in her new home, although she had eaten a large lunch. She did not know the meal's contents, remembering it was bland and unimaginative. Nonetheless, she ate it, placed the tray outside the door, and went straight to bed, hoping to have a long, deep, peaceful sleep.

Ellie was awakened at 6:30 the next morning by a centralized facility alarm system, a noise that sounded each morning thereafter to alert residents that breakfast was on its way. By 7:00 AM, breakfast was at her door. The meal consisted of oatmeal or dry cereal, alternating each day, with a small carton of milk and a piece of fresh fruit if they were lucky. But usually, dried or canned fruit was the featured fruit provided. The facility rarely served coffee because it was too expensive, since they imported most of it from other countries. If residents did not place their food trays back into the hallway by 8:00 AM, they would not receive a dinner meal. They never served lunch. A dinner alarm sounded at 4:30 PM. Dinner consisted of servings of a protein item, often beans; one carbohydrate item, usually pasta or potatoes; and one vegetable, generally canned and rarely fresh. The total daily calorie content averaged around 1000 calories per day. At this rate, Ellie would continue to lose weight, a process that began months ago as food supplies dwindled for everyone. She estimated she had lost close to 40 pounds; she had no spare fat tissue to burn.

For almost four months, Ellie spent most of her days listening to audiobooks, watching television with her peripheral vision, and taking walks in the long facility corridors. Residents would gather at a recreation area to tell stories of the good days long gone, discuss the prognosis of a better future, and gossip about the facility staff and other residents who declined this activity, including Ellie, who considered this form of entertainment thoroughly lacking mental stimulation. She had become very adept at providing her mental stimulation. However, she did spend more time than she should have trying to figure out what came next, preferring to focus on what was happening now.

Ellie also passed the time by walking the long corridors after dinner, remembering that this activity was good for burning off food sugar. But did that even matter at this point? The exercise always helped her mental attitude for a short while. About a week into this latest adventure, she bumped into a little old couple. Both were approximately 10 to 15 years older than her; the outgoing woman also had geographic atrophy, and he had dementia. Rather than split the couple up, the government let them reside together in the blind disability community. The three became fast friends who walked the corridors almost every evening, sharing life stories. He did not participate much in the conversation but interjected an alien comment occasionally. The two women shared a common spiritual awakening, revealing lectures they attended, teachers who guided them, and books they had read. Yes, they even discussed the book Mariah gave Ellie many years ago. Soon, the little man declined to go for the evening walk, leaving Ellie and the woman to explore each other's thoughts more deeply. These discussions helped them accept their fate, freed them from the unknown fear that fed their thoughts periodically, and strengthened their spiritual connection with the Creator. Ellie had finally received what she had wanted for decades—a soul mate to share a holy relationship with.

Four months after she arrived at the facility, a young man from the National Healthcare Administration came to visit her. As her assigned case worker, the young man, a degreed medical physician in residency, explained that he would escort her in a week to a clinic for a current examination and evaluation of her vision. He also informed her that the visit may require an overnight stay in the clinic and suggested she bring a few personal items. She hoped there would be enough room in the bag they provided to squeeze in the book Mariah gave her, which she always kept close by, although she could not see well enough to read it. It always provided spiritually manifested words to guide her through most events.

Epilogue

The knock on her apartment door jolted Ellie back into the present time. Looking at the clock on the table beside her chair, she noticed that she had been daydreaming for three hours. She slowly rose from the chair, sighed deeply, and walked to the door. But before she opened the door, she had one last impactful memory. Two years ago, she had asked a friend if she would accompany her on a trip to Arkansas to see her brother and his small family.

Since her friend had relatives in the area, she agreed to go on the journey to assist Ellie with navigating through the airport. Despite the transportation challenges they experienced during the trip, she had a lovely visit with her relatives—Lee, Sue, her nephew Alan, his wife Theresa, and their son Dawson. Just two years earlier, another nephew had passed away. This gathering occurred just before Christmas, so it was a sad time with such a notable absence. They enjoyed a week together, and then it was time for Ellie to return home and let the rest of the family enjoy their Christmas. While they waited at the flight departure gate, her friend entertained the family with stories Ellie had heard many times, so she slipped away from the group for a moment of peace. Swiftly, a wave of grief swept through her mind. Her eyes moistened as she thought this would be their last time together. The thought left as swiftly as it came; Ellie thanked God for the opportunity to be with all of them one more time.

The medical clinic was an hour's drive from her retirement community. As Ellie and her case worker approached the building, a sense of calmness swept over her. Nestled among trees and surrounded by shrubbery and beautiful flowers that she caught with her peripheral vision, the building was reminiscent of an estate belonging to someone who enjoyed unimagined wealth. An administrative staff member greeted them at the front door and escorted Ellie to her room on the second floor. What a beautiful sight to behold, recalling her home decades before life took Lundy from her. Because the day was coming to a close, a staff member instructed Ellie to make herself comfortable, and someone would come to escort her to the dining room at 7:00 PM for dinner.

Ellie was seated at a table for four; three other people were waiting for her arrival. They were visually handicapped as well, a bond that initiated conversation in the group. The other people had come to the clinic for the same reason as Ellie. Personal anxiety that they may have experienced disappeared as they discussed each other's lives. The dining room wait service was impeccable. The quality of the four-course dinner equaled that of the finest restaurants in Europe. Each diner embellished every bite of food and a swallow of each wine paired with each course. Before the group realized it, it was three hours later. Each one thanked the others for the pleasant evening, and the medical clinic staff escorted them back to their rooms.

Ellie's deep, peaceful sleep was interrupted by only one dream. In the dream, she participated in a movie she saw in her youth about a futuristic world in 2025, where the global situation was identical to what human beings were currently experiencing. The theme of the movie, Soylent Green, was the transformation of human bodies into food wafers called Soylent Green. A wake-up call from the front desk interrupted her thoughts about the dream, as she wondered what it was all about. Why did she suddenly recall the memory she had tucked into a hidden corner?

The staff attendant informed her that she could not eat breakfast in preparation for the fasting blood tests and series of eye examinations the following morning. At 9:00 AM, a medical attendant escorted her to the lab for blood draws, eye scanning device rooms, and an eye examination room. The attendant instructed her to go to the dining room for lunch. Then the attendant escorted her back for a consultation with the doctor at 2:00 PM. The doctor arrived a few minutes late to the meeting, but Ellie usually waited for doctors from every medical field.

The doctor informed her that the blood work results indicated that she would have no problem undergoing a new procedure, which could improve her vision. He told her that the medical staff would prepare her for the procedure. Ellie knew that research, including nanotechnology, was constantly being conducted to find a cure for macular degeneration. Within a few minutes, a nurse entered the room and instructed her to remove her clothes and change into a surgical gown.

A staff member escorted Ellie into a circular room with a surgical bed in the center surrounded by tables, trays, monitors, and medical equipment serving various purposes. She observed a bright light overhead. A series of dark windows at eye level from the bed encircled the room. The medical assistant explained that part of their procedure included the opportunity for the patient to listen to music. The music would have a calming effect on the patient during the procedure.

At their request, Ellie provided the title of her favorite song, which always induced a sense of peace and calm within her mind. A staff member instructed her to lie on the table and wait for the doctor to give her further instructions. The doctor came into the room and explained the process elements for the procedure: first, a staff member would start the music; next, the surgical staff would perform a final check of the required instruments and their proper location; then, they would administer the anesthetic, and finally, the doctor would perform the procedure.

As she waited for the music to begin, Ellie mentally laughed—maybe her final contribution to the world would be her reincarnation as a food wafer.

Music began to fill the room. The song was Silent Lucidity, written by Chris DeGarmo of the rock group Queensryche, which earned a Grammy award in 1992.

"Hush now, don't you cry
Wipe away the teardrop from your eye
You're lying safe in bed
It was all a bad dream spinning in your head

Your mind tricked you to feel the pain
Of someone close to you leaving the game of life
So here it is, another chance
Wide awake you face the day, your dream is over
Or has it just begun?

I will be watching over you
I am gonna help you see it through
I will protect you in the night
I am smiling next to you
In silent lucidity

If you open your mind for me
You won't rely on open eyes to see
The walls you built within
Come tumbling down, and a new world will begin."

Ellie's brain stopped receiving and translating the words.

- Event 7
Sight!

***